West of Me

A NOVEL BY
JAMIE GODFREY

Jamie Godfrey
202 Brunswick Street
Jersey City, NJ 07302

First edition: July 2013

Library of Congress Control Number: 2007012345

Godfrey, Jamie
      West of Me / Jamie Godfrey
      ISBN 978-0-578-12607-4

PRINTED IN THE UNITED STATES OF AMERICA

Contents

Welcome to my world.

Two Suitcases and $100

What did I get myself into? I asked myself as I looked out the airplane window. The New York skyline came into view. I had no idea how big it was. The grey buildings, tall and short, seemed to stretch out for miles in every direction. I sighed and sipped the last of my vodka from the plastic airplane cup. A few minutes later, I touched down on my new hometown.

I made my way through the airport and baggage claim and into a taxi. I had sweated through my shirt. Eight million people and I don't know one of them, I thought. My driver asked me something I couldn't make out so I just said yes. Moments later, I was standing on the corner of 27th and 7th, waiting in line to be checked into the dorms. It all happened so fast.

"Welcome," said a perky little dark haired girl, and then, pausing to look at a clipboard: "Kyle!" My God, I'm older than she is, I thought. It was true. I was not the traditional freshman as I had tried the whole college thing once before and it didn't stick. This time, at 23, it would be different. I was sure of it.

"Thank you," I said and she led me off in the direction of my new home. It was a giant concrete structure that looked more like a burned out, abandoned factory than dormitory.

"Where are you from?" she bubbled as we waited for the elevator.

"Wisconsin," I said with a smile.

"That's why you have that accent!" Oh, God. *Did* I? I thought. Now I was going to be self-conscious every time I spoke. "Here you go!" she said, getting off on the 15th floor. My door was the first door to the right of the elevators. She handed me the key and welcomed me again.

Inside, I found butter-colored glossy walls that had been painted over at least six times, hair and dust trapped in the layers. There was a kitchen with appliances as old as I was and fake wood cabinets with the edges peeling. Then there was the main room. That room was full of light, big and open, with two beds, two desks and a table and chairs and plenty of room for personal effects. I took the bed closest to the bathroom and moved the desk directly in front of the windows so I could look out.

First thing I did was unpacked my PowerBook and connected it to the Internet. "I made it!" I wrote all my friends and family. Typing that sentence made me cry, realizing that I was now 800 miles away from them and on a completely different path. There I was, alone, in New York City, at the Fashion Institute of Technology to study Fashion Design. Even after graduation, there wouldn't probably be much for me back in Wisconsin.

"Hey!" a voice boomed from the hall.

"Hi!" I said as my roommate Jim, rounded the corner and shook my hand. He was the whitest person I had ever met. He was tall, pale and had strawberry blond hair and tons of freckles. He was from upstate New York, there to study Graphic Design. He set up his stuff as I chatted with his parents. They definitely had accents, not me.

His parents kissed him good-bye and we both sat on our beds staring at one another, wondering what to do next.

We both turned and logged on our computers. Living with Jim was like having a pet I didn't have to take care of. He was there for quiet companionship, but I didn't have to walk him or feed him or pet him. And if anything happened to him, it wasn't on me. We were a good match for roommates. We were both quiet, on our computers most of the time, slept in late, stayed up late and pretty much felt that the world dropped off in a two block radius around campus.

We went to freshmen orientation together and sat through a poorly acted skit about the dangers of college drinking. This is hardly going to deter me, I thought, thinking of the bottle of Beaujolais in my desk. "I'll buy you dinner," Jim offered. I accepted. We went to McDonald's across the street. Not what I had in mind, but it was a meal.

Draping 101 was the following day. True to form, I was early. I sat at a cork-lined worktable on a stainless steel stool, surrounded by dress forms, waiting for my professor and peers to arrive. People began trickling in and quietly taking their spots.

"I don't want the fat girl!" pouted one girl who was forced to take the size 10 form instead of the 8's the rest of us had.

Then, this larger than life, tattoo-covered girl with bright blue hair and ear, eye and nose rings came in, carrying way too many bags for the first day. Everything crashed down as she dropped her totes on the table. "Who you callin' fat?" she barked with a slight, Southern drawl. I was immediately terrified of her.

Our professor, Mrs. Whitford, arrived a few minutes later. She was the Italian Fran Drescher. Looked like her, spoke like her. She had us all in tears laughing within in minutes. Maybe this was going to be ok, I thought.

After class, I packed up my bag and started walking towards the door when I heard the girl with the blue hair talking to the person next to her. "I have no fucking clue what I'm doing."

Without thinking, I blurted: "I can help you."

"Really?" she said.

"Yeah. I'm in the dorms. I could come by. I'm on 15."

"Me too!"

"Really? Cool. Are you free at 7? I can come by and we can figure this out together." And with that, it was settled. Before our scheduled time, I ran across the street to the bodega and took two Budweiser 40's from the cooler and set them on the counter. I took out the $100 bill from my wallet, all the money I had.

I knocked on the blue haired girl's door and held up the beers as she opened it.

"I love you," she whispered, putting her hand over her heart. I handed her a beer and walked in her room. We sat down at her table and began drinking.

"I realized I don't even know your name," I said.

"Sydney Smutts."

"I'm Kyle Meyers."

"King of Beers!" she said.

"King of Queers!" I retorted and she spit out her beer all over her muslin.

Sydney's very manly looking roommate, Tina, threw open the front door. "Is anyone in the shitter? I need to take a duke."

"Seriously?" I said and Sydney busted out laughing. Day one wasn't so bad. I could only imagine what adventures were in store for me ahead.

Cold Beer Deli

"I'm hungry," Sydney said as we sat around her table in the dorm apartment.

"We just had dinner an hour ago," I said, even though I was just as hungry. Let's be real. I can always eat. "What do you want?"

"A cheese sandwich from Cold Beer Deli."

"What the hell is Cold Beer Deli?"

"You don't know? Let's go." Cold Beer Deli. Its moniker came from the blinking neon sign that hung above its front door. It was just around the corner from FIT, so it easily became our go-to spot for food. It was your garden variety NYC bodega. It had shelves of dust-covered cans of soup, one-ply toilet paper and a cold cuts case that always had a container of Mayo with a crust across it.

Most notably, they had the best selection of 40's on the planet. There was, of course, Colt 45 and Olde English, but there were other favorites like Country Club and one that was simply named Beer in block letters (that one was always a last resort). The best part was that they were all under three dollars. For a budget college drinker, this was like winning the lottery.

The establishment was run by three brothers of Middle Eastern descent. They were extremely kind and welcoming. I never did learn their names, but they certainly knew ours. The mascot of the place was this black cat that had free reign. I often thought that they were breaking at least a handful of health codes by having him there, but he was sweet and I never found cat hair in the food.

Sydney introduced me to the equivalent of deli crack: the cheese sandwich. In theory it was simple. The sandwich consisted of a roll, slices of provolone, cheddar, Swiss, mustard (Never the crusty Mayo. Two girls on our floor got violent food poisoning from it) and lettuce. That's it, but it was magical. Crave worthy. And it too, was under three dollars.

Back in Sydney's dorm apartment, we enjoyed our cheese sandwiches and washed them down with beer. We took the caps of the 40's and pressed them into the ceiling. We eventually made a happy face out of them. Sydney's mascot was this girl named Caryn, whom she met at orientation, who never left Sydney's room. She was always there, lying on the floor, flipping through old copies of *Betty Crocker* cookbooks. I don't think I ever saw her actually cook anything, but she was always there reading.

"Does she ever leave?" I asked setting my 40 down on the table.

"I don't even notice anymore."

"Does she at least cook for you?"

"No. She just reads cookbooks for fun."

"Weird." I was watching her circle recipes and study the illustrations intently. I was studying her so intently, I wasn't watching where I was setting my 40 and then it spilled. Everywhere. Actually, it was mainly on Sydney's Italian textbook.

"Kyle!" she screamed at me. I was more worried about the fallen malt liquor than her book. She ran to the kitchen to retrieve a towel, but the damage was done. It was soaked.

"What happened?" said Jim, as he entered. From day one, he took a liking to me. We're talking *Single White Female* style. He hung out with my friends, followed me around campus like a lost puppy, and he even cut his hair just like mine. At first, I thought it was flattering and then it just became annoying. I worked hard to cultivate my pack of friends and my identity and didn't want someone just swooping in and capitalizing on all that work.

"Kyle spilled his beer all over Sydney's book," said Caryn, not looking up from her cookbook.

"Sweet," he said as he sat down, not realizing that the chair was covered with beer. "Oh, man!" he said jumping back up. We all roared with laughter. Except Sydney, who was frantically wiping up beer.

I often thought that Jim and Caryn should hook up. They both had the same level of freak factor that would make them a pair. Alas, Jim continued dating this girl from back home who was clearly a lesbian.

"Where's your girlfriend?" I asked.

"She's fixing her truck."

Wow, I thought. Jim pulled out a notebook and began sketching what looked to be a super hero. "Caryn and Jim should pen a super hero cookbook," I mused. I really needed to let it go, they weren't going to be a couple.

For a solid two years, Sydney and I would frequent the deli for sandwiches and beer. Then, one night as we were leaving class, we noticed billows of smoke in the direction of Cold Beer Deli. We ran to find it engulfed in flames, dozens of firefighters trying to put out the blaze. We stood there silently, watching our little sandwich heaven glowing orange. Almost as a reflex, Sydney and I joined hands.

Not taking her eyes off the fire, she said: "Thanks to you, my Italian professor thinks I'm an alcoholic. Gave me a pamphlet about going to A.A." I was too in shock to laugh (later, I did).

Our beloved deli was gone. The brothers were arrested for having started the fire in the hopes of cashing in the insurance policy on the place. For years, we tried to recreate that sandwich. Sometimes at home, sometimes at other bodegas. Never with any success.

"I hope the cat is ok," I said.

You're Not My Type #1

I had a crush on Henry. There. I said it. I looked forward to my Monday morning draping class, if only to be able to see him. I positioned my dress form so I could be in perfect view of him. He was of Eastern European descent. Or at least his grandparents or someone was. He was thin, pale skin, jet black hair that kind of did whatever it wanted and some days he wore thick black-framed glasses that sat atop of a big, thin nose. He was quiet, gentle and soft-spoken. There was something about him that was absolutely magnetic. I couldn't wait to hear him speak in class, look over his sketches and watch him work. I tried, whenever I could, to stand next to him.

"Why don't you ask him out?" Sydney said, pinning muslin to her dress form.

"I can't do that."

"Why not?"

"I'm too nervous. And he's too shy. The whole thing would be too awkward."

"I'll do it," she said with a devil-may-care attitude, taking a pin from her mouth and placing into the form.

"Are we on the playground?"

"Well, I'm tired of watching you watch him."

"He's so pretty."

"I'm going to do it," she said. When Sydney had something in her head, it was as good as done. Rather than fight her, I worked with her to develop a plan for her asking Henry out for me. I was to get up and go to the bathroom when Henry's friends had left him to work. I didn't want them overhearing Sydney asking him and then it becoming a giant production and embarrassment for me.

I was going to stand outside the door and listen to their conversation. I didn't tell Sydney this part.

Finally, the moment came. Henry's friends had taken a break to go get sodas. I nodded at Sydney that the plan was in motion and took my leave. I stood directly outside the draping room door.

"Hey, Henry," Sydney approached him.

"Hey, how's it going?" he asked, continuing to pin grey flannel fabric to the form.

"Listen, I have a question for you. You know Kyle right?"

"Of course."

"He really, really likes you. Would you be interested in going out with him?"

He stopped his work and turned to face her. "He's a really great guy, don't get me wrong. He's just not my type." Sydney nodded and returned to her pinning. I texted her: "Heard the convo. Not coming back to class. Bring my stuff to my room."

Help Me!

Comfort food has always been high on my list when it comes to food choices. Meatloaf, chicken and waffles, beef stew, spaghetti and meatballs and of course, the ultimate comfort food, chicken potpie. And I was craving it. For Christmas, my mom had bought me *Marsha Stuart's Comfort Food Cookbook* (we'll call her that as you will later see why) and I was dying to cook from it.

When I arrived at FIT, I thought I was going to be in a standard dorm room. When I got checked in, I discovered that I had been upgraded to a dorm apartment. Had I known I was going to have a full kitchen, I would have arrived with more than just two suitcases of clothing and my PowerBook. Nevertheless, being slightly older than the average freshman, it was a pleasant surprise to be able to live more like an adult while going to school.

List in hand, I went to the market and collected the necessary ingredients. This was going to be the most expensive meal I had had in ages, but it was worth it to satiate the craving. Returning to the apartment, I realized that I was missing a very crucial ingredient to this process: a stockpot.

I banged on Sydney's door. "What?" she said opening it and rubbing her eyes.

"It's 3 p.m.! Wake up!"

"Late night," she said, holding the door for me.

"Apparently. Listen, do you have a stockpot I can borrow?"

"Sure," she said, going into the kitchen and getting it for me. "What are you making?"

"Chicken potpie," I said as she yanked the pot back out of my hands. "What?"

"I don't want your death in my pot." Sydney was a devout vegetarian. This was a problem.

"I'll wash it!"

"Still. The death will be in the pot."

"Fine," I said with a huff and took my leave, going directly back to the market where, luckily, they had a cheap quality, overpriced stockpot.

With Coltrane playing on iTunes, I chopped vegetables, made chicken stock, rolled out pastry dough. Heaven. When all the components came together and were in the oven, I started to clean up. I looked at the chicken carcass in my new stockpot and busted out laughing. I knew what to do with it.

Perched upon a plate, I took the carcass down the hall and set it in front of Sydney's door with a sticky note on it that read: HELP ME!

Back in my apartment, blanketed in the perfume of baking goodness, I took the potpie out of the oven and cut a piece. I sat down at the table, which I rarely ate at, and did it properly, with a napkin and candles and jazz. I was midway into my meal when I could hear "KY-LE!" vibrating through the walls. I smiled. You're welcome, I thought.

Employees Must Wash Hands

Sydney and I stumbled upon *Buon Gusto* quite by accident. We had ditched our afternoon patternmaking class in search of booze. We wanted to find a place that was close to school, but tucked away enough that the annoying Fashion Merchandising girls wouldn't frequent it. *Buon Gusto* was that place.

Half was a restaurant and the other was a bar and lounge. The entire space had exposed brick walls that had been painted a dark maroon color. Giant gold frame mirrors lined the back of the bar and red shaded sconces dotted the wall opposite. It felt very seedy and bohemian. The restaurant looked more VFW hall than fine eatery with its wooden Formica tables and vinyl padded banquet chairs. We were in love.

Sydney and I sat down at the bar. We were the only people in there. Well, it was 3 p.m. after all. Kelly, a tall, platinum blond, dressed head to toe in black sauntered over to us. "What can I get you?" she asked, sans smile. Radiohead played in the background.

"Jack and Coke for me," said Sydney.

"Campari and soda for me," I followed.

"You want to pay now or start a tab?"

"We can start a tab." I pulled out my wallet to hand Kelly my bankcard and a shiny metal object followed with.

"What's that?" Sydney inquired.

"It's a compass my friend Jan gave me before leaving Wisconsin to come here. It's so I will never lose my way."

"Aww! That's so sweet." Upon further inspection, Sydney discovered it was permanently stuck to the west. "It's broken."

"Yeah, I know. I like the sentiment behind it, so I keep it."

Our drinks arrived. We sat a while in silence, enjoying our discovery.

"You two go to FIT?" asked Kelly, taking a drag from her cigarette, hand on her hip, still no smile.

"Yeah, we're Fashion Design majors," Sydney answered for the two of us.

"I went there. Fine Arts. Painting. Graduated last year."

"So, you know the lay of the land," I said, which was met with a nod and another drag of her cigarette.

"Don't you dare tell anyone about this place," she ordered, pointing at us. Stunned, both Sydney and I shook our heads. "The last thing we want is those Fashion Merchandising girls in here. Can't stand those bitches." We busted out laughing and said the secret was safe with us.

A few drinks later, the place as brimming with regulars. Mainly gruff, surly guys who worked up the block at the TV studio where a couple trashy daytime talk shows were taped. Kelly took their shit and fed it right back to them. The room was full of smoke, laughter and Pearl Jam. The place was perfect for us.

Finally, the time came for me to use the men's room. It was up five steps in the back of the bar, which can be dangerous after a few drinks. The bathroom was the smallest bathroom in the world. It had a toilet and a sink and no space in between. When you were done peeing, you only had to pivot to the right a little and there was the sink. While washing my hands, I spied the "Employees Must Wash Hands Before Returning to Work" sign. I noticed the corner of it was coming off from the wall, so I helped it along, releasing it to freedom and slid it up my shirtsleeve to deposit in Sydney's lap as a gift.

Each week we would return and the same scenario would play out: we would have drinks, I would get tipsy and end up in the bathroom and peel the sign off the wall. The sign I took the previous week would always be replaced by a shiny new one. The signs varied in font and layout, which was nice. The owner must have had several sources to purchase them from.

Back in her apartment, Sydney completely tiled the walls of her bathroom with the signs. Which was good because the owner started writing the directive on a piece of white paper with a Sharpie. Which of course, I didn't take.

You've Got Mail

My cube was lined with the ubiquitous, nubbly grey fabric that I avoided touching with my life. I knew there were colonies of undiscovered parasites living in those slubs. I looked around my 4x4 cell and thought: this is like a casino, but without the fun and free drinks. Or prison. At least there, you get a window.

My internship at R.A.G. (Reynolds Apparel Group) was boring, to say the least. I spent my days surfing the Internet and chatting with friends. In the off chance there was something to do, I spent my time opening shipments, measuring plus sized track suits and tacky sweaters and noted them on a log. Was this the life I was going to lead after graduation? I shuddered.

Just when I thought I had visited every single website in existence, an idea struck. Tapping into a higher power, I decided to sign Sydney up for anything and everything free. You name it, I signed her up for it. Adult diapers, VHS tapes on choosing the right RV, hemorrhoid cream, baby formula (she doesn't have a baby), Book of Mormon (she's an atheist), mouthwash, college applications, every catalog in existence, dog food (she doesn't have a dog), tampons, breathe right strips, vacation planning brochures, power tools DVD, laundry detergent, condoms, zero-calorie sweeteners, razors, diabetic cookbooks (she's not diabetic), beef jerky, personal lubricant, mobility scooter videos, coloring books, antacids, shampoo, protein bars, shaving cream, organic seeds, temporary Jesus tattoos, carpet tiles. I found my calling.

I busted out laughing every time I clicked send. Suddenly, I didn't mind going in to work three times a week after school, when my friends were either sleeping or shopping. I was giddy at the thought of Sydney coming home to a pile of mail and wondering why she was suddenly getting skin cancer screenings and gun safety DVDs.

I told our receptionist Betty about my plan. "You're evil," she said with a smile. She was this tiny, little thing with bright orange hair, but was as fiery as they come. I was petrified of her when I first met her, but soon we were fast friends. I got in trouble once for standing at the front desk talking to her, so we moved our clandestine meetings to the supply closet. There we would talk about our dieting attempts and American Idol.

"I love the smell of markers," I said as I pulled the cap off and huffed one. Betty followed suit.

"Does nothing for me. I grew up in the 60's, remember."

"Speaking of, what did you think of Idol last night?"

"I like when they sing current songs. It seemed unnatural for them to sing oldies."

"I guess," I said, putting the cap back on the marker.

"What is Sydney going to do with all those samples?"

"I don't know, but I can't wait to see her expression."

"You better not send me anything," she said in her stern, motherly voice. I flashed her an evil grin.

For the better part of three weeks, I scoured the Internet for freebies. It even spilled over into my free time. Before class, I'd pour a cup of coffee and start signing her up. On the weekend, I would continue the search. After exhausting the free samples, I began signing her up for coupons, newsletters and free subscriptions.

"Did you do this?" said Sydney as she entered the draping studio, holding a maxi-pad and a pack of gum.

I stopped pinning muslin to the dress form and busted out laughing.

"I knew it! And my inbox is full. I spent an hour this morning just deleting emails." I almost fell off my stool. "I hate you!" she said throwing the maxi-pad at me.

"You'll thank me! Some of those samples are good. I even sent a few to myself."

"My mailbox was so crammed full of catalogs, I had to rip the L.L. Bean catalog into shreds to wedge the rest free." I howled with laughter. She took her muslin out of her bag and put it on the form.

"I...love...you," I said in a pouty voice. She finally cracked a smile.

Eventually the sign-ups died off and I waited for her to tell me of her spoils. Every day she would give me the update as to what arrived. Each day, the volume increasing.

"Look at this," she said holding up a very official letter.

Dear Rev. Sydney Xena Smutts, of the Smutts Center for Vaginal Dryness,

Due to the volume of mail you are receiving on a daily basis, we cannot accommodate home delivery for you. We will hold your mail at the Warren Street post office location for you to pick up.

We appreciate your business and cooperation.

Sincerely,
Ruth Brown

"I'm a reverend? My middle name is now Xena? And I run a center on vaginal dryness?" she said trying to hold back a smile.

"I thought you would like that touch."

"I have to pick up my own mail now! I had to take a granny cart with me to haul it home." I was crying I was laughing so hard.

"Get anything good?" I choked.

"I do like the informational Glenlivet whiskey video."

Over the next six months she continued to pile on the free samples. Gone was her need to buy dish soap, toothpaste or dryer sheets. Often, we would get drunk and watch the Craftmatic bed video with this cartoon sheep that would "Baaa" across the screen at the oddest intervals. We watched it so many times, the tape eventually broke. She then made a conceptual art piece out of all those VHS tapes. She's moved nine times and changed her email twice. They still find her.

You're Not My Type #2

I was sitting at my internship, feeling rather horny. It was Friday night, I had no plans and it had been ages since, well, as Blanche from *Golden Girls* would have put it, enjoyed the company of a man. Knowing that my success with the bar scene less than stellar, I took to the Internet to procure me a man.

I found a guy named Jimmy. He was a few years younger than me, worked at MTV, not far from my internship, had his own place and agreed to meet me after work. Score! I raced through measuring these Christmas sweatshirts with appliqué snowmen and reindeer on them. While tacky, they reminded me of home. The ladies wearing them at holiday time, over solid color turtlenecks, as they shopped for ingredients to make ambrosia salad. I shuddered.

With my time sheet complete, I said good-bye to Betty and wished her a restful weekend. Jimmy and I had agreed to meet in Times Square, just outside the Viacom/MTV building. I would recognize him from his photo, but if that didn't work, he was wearing a baby blue dress shirt and grey dress pants. I was confident I would pull him out of the crowd.

There he was. Thin, curly chocolate brown hair, Ray-Ban sunglasses. He was beautiful. "Hi," I said and we awkwardly shook hands. "Hi," he replied.

"Well, how do you want this to work?" I asked nervously, wishing he would take his sunglasses off so I could see his eyes. I bet they were beautiful.

"Um, let's start walking."

"Ok," I said and started following him westward to the fringes of Times Square, where the old naughty movie stores moved when Times Square got cleaned up. We didn't speak. It was incredibly awkward, but nevertheless, I followed him like a lost puppy.

We came upon a store that had just the word ADULT flashing in lights and some scary mannequins wearing only fishnet stockings in the window. "Let's get a movie," he said with a smile. I was never really into porn and had never found myself in need of visiting such an establishment. Why not? I thought.

Rows and rows of videos for whatever it is you're into lined the space. I could only imagine what went on in the booths in the back of the store. I nervously picked up a few titles and put them immediately back. Jimmy apparently seemed to know the layout of the store and already had a few DVDs in his hand. "What are you into?" he asked. I glanced at the movies he selected, which included: *Black Cock Down*, *Shaving Ryan's Privates* and *Military Discharge*. I guess I knew what he was into.

"I'm sure those are fine," I said. He paid for the movies and we left. He in his sunglasses and me in his wake.

Street after street, I followed him awkwardly and without saying anything. I made a few attempts at conversation, but nothing that spurred a discussion or follow-up. I made a couple of attempts at touching him, nudging him with my arm, patting him on the back. Nothing was returned.

Block by block, this went on. We were now below 14th Street. I had no idea where I was. I thought he said he lived in Chelsea. Oh, well. The weather was great, it was

Friday night and I was being led back to the house of a very hot hookup. Life was good. Who cares if we had nothing to speak about? That wasn't the point of us being together!

We came to his apartment. It was reminiscent of the brownstone used in *Sex and the City*. "Well," he said nervously, "This is it."

"Very nice. Shall we go in?" I asked, trying to make out his eyes behind his sunglasses. There was a very long and drawn out pause. I think he was hoping I would 'get it' without him having to spell it out for me. But, I wasn't giving up. We agreed to do this and I was present to do so.

"Look," he started as my heart began its ride down to my stomach. "I'm going to go in alone."

"Why?" Oh, dear God, why did I ask why?

"You're just not my type." With that, I turned, not saying good-bye and started my walk back home. I had no idea where I was, so, I tried to backtrack the way I came.

It being Friday night and now with no plans, I decided to do the only thing a person in my situation should do: drink. I really hoped that Kelly would be working at *Buon Gusto*. I really didn't feel like drinking alone in my room. Luckily, she was.

"How are you?" I asked as I sat down at the far end of the bar. For a Friday night, it was surprisingly empty. Was it a holiday I didn't know about?

"I'm bleeding like I got shot in the crotch. You?" She took a drag from her cigarette and swept her platinum blond hair behind her ear.

"Wow," I said as she took a double old fashioned glass and filled it with ice and Campari and soda. "Actually, I was just stood up. Well, not stood up so much as I was told I'm not his type."

"Drink's on me." She waived my wallet back into my pants. She never comp'd drinks. Ever. Mainly because the owner watched her like a hawk. Maybe he needed the money to replace all those signs I took from the bathroom.

"What's the occasion?"

"You had a shitty day and I had a good one. I sold a painting."

"That's fantastic! To whom?"

"An art collector." I smiled. It was nice to hear good news. Even though it didn't involve me getting it on with a hot guy. She watched my face drop as I turned back to my drink and she said: "You want anything to eat? I get a meal per shift and I ate before I got here. I'll give it to you." I smiled.

The food at *Buon Gusto* was incredible. As the name suggests, it served Italian fare. Sydney had turned me on to spinach tortellini in Alfredo sauce. It was out of this world good. That's what I ordered. While I waited for my pasta, Kelly brought me a basket of focaccia bread. Quietly, I poured olive oil onto a plate and dabbed the bread in it. I may not have gotten laid, but at least I got fed.

Full Service

I sat at my desk, looking out over the buildings surrounding 26th street. My dorm apartment had the good fortune of being on the 15th floor and the building adjacent was only a couple stories tall. I sat at my computer, procrastinating and watching the people across the way, *Rear Window* style. There was the nudist, the elderly couple, the massage school, and the requisite artist. They were my friends I never met.

I clicked play on Wynton Marsalis in iTunes and studied my friends. Nothing too interesting, but I nevertheless couldn't take my eyes off of them. Pausing, to pour a glass of wine, I saw an email come through from Daniel.

Daniel and I had spoken online, but hadn't officially met. We had exchanged a handful of playful emails and then swapped photos. There was attraction on both sides. Success. Now it was just up to meeting. The dreaded meeting.

> *Kyle,*
>
> *Hey you. You hungry?*
>
> *D.*

Of course I was hungry. Duh!

> *Ravenous,* I playfully replied.
>
> *Gramercy Tavern in an hour?*

Daniel was something of a foodie. I was too, at heart, but my student checking account thought differently. My focus drifted back to the massage school. There were five people lying under sheets, getting their shoulders and upper backs rubbed. Maybe I should volunteer there, I thought as I rubbed a knot in my right shoulder blade.

My treat, bounced in another email from him, prodding me to commit.

See you there.

With that, I got up and went to my closet. It screamed broke student. I pulled out an old Banana Republic dress shirt and set up the ironing board. Don't screw this up, I thought as I sprayed starch on the yoke. Daniel was a med student at NYU. He had sandy blond hair, like me, and fair features. He had a very kind face. I often thought, if he were my doctor, I would feel at ease if he entered the room and had to deliver bad news. It just seemed easier coming from that face.

I tucked my shirt into my dress pants and pulled on my grey and black herringbone blazer. Dressed up enough, but casual enough to not be stuffy. I took the last swig of wine and hid the empty bottle back in my desk drawer. Legally, I could drink, but not on campus. This didn't dissuade me in the least from sneaking in wine, vodka, or grain alcohol at any chance I got.

I got on the elevator as my R.A. was getting off. Oh, shit, I thought. Do I smell like wine? She said good night and put the key in her lock. I think I dodged that bullet.

The night air had a chill to it. I wished I had grabbed a scarf on the way out the door. I put my hands in my pockets and began walking over to the restaurant. A million thoughts circled around in my head. What if he has bad breath? What if we have nothing to talk about in person? I've always wanted to be the wife of a doctor. This could be my chance.

There he was. Standing outside the restaurant, looking as nervous I felt, bouquet of tulips in hand.

"Kyle!" he exclaimed and opened his arms.

"Daniel!" I exclaimed, falling into his embrace. He smelled good.

"Let's eat!" he said and hopped over and opened the door and handed me the flowers, all in one gesture. I smiled and walked through. Judging by his enthusiasm, we are off to a great start. No bad breath and a level of mutual excitement. All I could ask for. "You don't mind that we have a table in the bar area, do you? I couldn't get us into the restaurant."

"I don't care! It's just great to be with you," I said. He smiled and touched my arm.

He pulled my chair out and tucked me in like a perfect gentleman. My gentle doctor with the kind face. I sighed, smiled and opened my menu.

Celery root chowder with mussels, clams and ham. Sure beats the leftover cafeteria chicken sandwich I had planned feasting on. Butternut squash lasagna with kale and pinenuts? Sign me up.

Our waiter approached the table. A dashing guy, around our age with a closely trimmed beard, piercing blue eyes and a confidence I could only dream of possessing. "Hi, my name is Nick, I'll be your server tonight." Daniel was locked in his gaze. "Can I start you off with something to drink?"

"I'll have a gin martini," said Daniel, not looking away from Nick.

"I'll have a Campari and soda," I said, interrupting their locked eyes.

"Great," Nick said and dashed away, patting Daniel gently on the shoulder as he did.

"So," I started, a little shaken. "How's your exam prep going?"

"Intense, but good. Thank you for offering me a break from it," he said taking a sip of his water. "What about you?"

"My final is to design a garment based on my favorite fruit. For me, it's blueberries. But, I have no idea how I'm going to do that. I want to do something less obvious than blue and purple beads." I couldn't help but notice his gaze was at Nick, behind the bar, making our drinks.

"I'm sure it will be great," he said, finally, turning my way.

"It's so great to finally meet you! I don't know why we didn't meet sooner!" I said.

"Yes, it is great to put a face with the emails."

Nick returned. Oh, chiseled Nick.

"Have you given any thought to what you would like? Perhaps I could recommend something," he said, directly to Daniel. It was very clear that I wouldn't be getting any recommendations from Nick.

"I'd love the Arctic Char," Daniel said. Nick flashed him a smile and scribbled it on his pad.

"And for you?" Nick asked, again, not looking at me.

"I'll have the lasagna."

"Great!" he said, patting Daniel on the shoulder again as he walked away.

Daniel could see the worry on my face and immediately tried to reassure me. "You look very nice."

"Thank you," I replied awkwardly. I could see Nick at the computer entering our order. He kept looking over at Daniel. Suddenly, I felt like a contestant on a really, really bad reality show. Was this really happening? Why?! "Thank you for the flowers. They're lovely."

"You are very welcome." He smiled a beautiful smile. "I remember you mentioning that you really like white tulips."

"I do." I was seriously at a loss. How could I compete with Nick? This was clearly going south fast. And speaking of, there he was returning to our table with bread.

"Thank you," Daniel said, staring up at Nick. We both reached for the bread at the same time. Our hands met in what should have been a romantic gesture straight from the movies, but he didn't acknowledge it. "What do you do outside of waiting tables?"

"I'm an actor. Well, I'm trying to be."

"Trying!? Either you are or you aren't!" quipped Daniel.

"Well, then, it's official. I am an actor," he said, bowing slightly in. I felt like I was watching a movie. A surreal, unfortunate movie while I snacked on carbs. This train was officially off the tracks, full steam ahead.

"Are you starring in anything currently?" inquired Daniel.

"Yeah, I'm staring as George in my department's production of *Hedda Gabler*."

"I love Ibsen! What school do you go to?"

"NYU."

"No way! Me too. Pre-med."

"Awesome." They continued to smile at one another. I continued to feed myself torn bits of bread. They continued to hold their gaze. "Listen, if you'd like to come, I'll get you a ticket."

"I'd love that."

Wow, I thought, continuing to tear the slices into bits and pop them in my mouth. In my mind I was stabbing Nick a thousand times in the face.

"Here's my number," said Nick as he scribbled it onto a scrap of paper. Daniel took it from him with the biggest smile. After Nick had left, he turned and remembered I was sitting there. The smile dropped from his face and he picked up a piece of bread.

"Thanks for the flowers," I said as I stood up and walked to the door.

I walked back to the dorms, slower that I normally do, lost inside my head. I passed a little bitty thing of an old lady with a hair bonnet and orthopedic shoes, pushing a granny cart full of groceries.

"Here," I offered her the tulips. "For you."

Jack

Skipping life drawing class (who really wants to sketch an 80 year old naked woman for three hours, from every angle?), I ended up at *Buon Gusto*. As luck would have it, Kelly was tending bar.

"Sup?" she asked, cigarette hanging from the corner of her mouth as she washed glasses in the sink behind the bar. She was dressed in her signature all black.

"Nothing." She set an ice-filled glass in front of me and instinctually poured me a Campari and soda.

"Skipping class, I see."

"Ok, Mom," I said sarcastically.

"Your creepy roommate was in here earlier looking for you."

"Of course he was." Damn. Now he's discovered my *Buon Gusto*. "What did you say?"

"I told him to get the fuck out." I choked back a laugh.

"Anything new?" I asked, as she took a drag from her cigarette.

"Nah, nothing. Say, you been stealing the signs from the bathroom? My boss is real mad." Oh shit, I thought.

"Nope, wasn't me," I said. I could feel my face turning red. I was such a bad liar. It was always blatantly obvious when I was doing it. Still haven't perfected it, despite years of practice.

Just then, the most beautiful man I had ever seen entered. "Hey, are you Paul?" he asked me. I couldn't stop staring at him.

"No, Paul's in the back. Who are you?" Kelly asked.

"Jack," he said. I melted.

"Let me get him for you."

"Jack," he said, extending his hand to mine. He had wavy jet-black hair, pale skin, doe-y brown eyes, thick black glasses, nerdy and skinny.

"Kyle," I said, not wanting to let go of his hand.

"Yeah, I'm playing here tonight."

"What do you play?" I asked nervously. It was very obvious as he was carrying a guitar case.

"Guitar. And I sing. All my own, original stuff." Instantly, I knew what my evening plans were. "What do you do, Kyle?"

"I'm a student at FIT. Fashion Design."

"Very cool. I don't know much about fashion," he said tugging at his ratty-looking Journey T-shirt. He smiled and I was a pile of goo. I couldn't have dreamt a more beautiful man than Jack. And the thing is, I don't think he even realized how beautiful he was. Kelly returned with

Paul and they went in the back, to discuss the particulars of him performing there.

"He's hot!" I exclaimed.

"He's straight," said Kelly, resuming her glass washing.

"Of course he is," I said and tapped my drink for her to pour another. "They all are."

Jack returned to set up his stand and equipment in the little space between the bar and the front door. I moved a seat down so I would have prime viewing of him. I watched him as he took his guitar out of its case, arranged his set list and music on the stand, turned his guitar, never taking my eyes off of him. Please God, at least let him be bi or curious. Or both.

Eventually, the bar was full and Jack began his set. He had the most heavenly voice. It matched his beautiful face and his gentle nature. I stayed for the full set. I even stayed to watch him pack up his gear. "See you round," he waved to me as he left. I settled my tab, said good night to Kelly, who shook her head at me, and left. The cool air felt good on my skin as I walked back to the dorms. I couldn't get Jack's voice out of my head. Not that I really wanted to. I felt like a piece of me that was missing had momentarily been found.

The next day, I went back to *Buon Gusto* and got his schedule from Kelly. I made certain to be present for each of his performances. I even bought his demo CD from him. He insisted that I have it for free, but I said that all artists should be compensated for their work, to help them keep creating art. He hugged me. I felt a jolt of electricity shock through my body.

The night before Thanksgiving, I was all alone at *Buon Gusto*. So was Kelly. She comp'd me my usual spinach tortellini, focaccia bread and a drink. "Happy Thanksgiving," I said to her. "I'd much rather be here with you than with my family."

"Amen," she said, taking a shot of some amber colored liquor, followed by a drag from her cigarette. Just then, Jack walked through the door and sat down next to me.

"Kyle! No turkey day plans?" he asked.

"No, I am staying put this holiday. I'll be home in a few weeks for Christmas." He and Kelly made eye contact.

"I'll have a whiskey sidecar," he said. In all the weeks I had been here with him, I never recalled him ordering a drink, much less such an old school one. "Yeah, I'm not doing anything for Thanksgiving either."

"We should do Thanksgiving together," I blurted out, immediately turning bright red at not having thought this through.

"Sure!" he said, defying what I thought would be his expected response.

"Is there anything you don't like to eat?"

"Nah, I'll eat pretty much anything." It was settled. He would come over my apartment and I would make Thanksgiving. Shit, I thought, I need to hustle. I bet everything had already been sold out at the market.

I gave him my cell number and chugged my drink. Kelly tossed me a look that said 'you're wasting your time!' And I knew I was. He was straight. That was obvious. But, he was so beautiful and talented and the nicest guy I'd met.

At the market, I just started throwing things in my cart that I thought I would need to make a Thanksgiving dinner. Chicken stock, stuffing mix, celery, onions, carrots, potatoes, garlic, a 20 pound turkey (I know, for 2 people), green beans, cornbread (the bread selection at this point was next to nothing), and I knew I wouldn't have time to bake so I snagged the last pumpkin pie on the bakery shelf. Shit, I should have invited Kelly. I texted her.

Kelly: No, thank you. He's str8!

Yeah, yeah, Kelly. I know. But, that doesn't bother me. Back at my apartment, I began the prep. The dinner was the following day and had never done it before. I assembled the stuffing in a baking dish I got on sale at Fishs Eddy, peeled the potatoes and set them in water in the fridge, trimmed and cleaned the green beans and even brined the turkey. I didn't have much in my fridge to begin with, so putting a turkey in there to brine was no problem. After this was set, I went to Bed Bath and Beyond got a set of tea-lights and stopped by the bodega and got rust-colored mums to put on the table.

Back in my room, I had some extra fabric left over from a project so I made napkins and placemats for us. I set the table, flowers in the center and tea-lights in little clear glass votives from IKEA all around the table and all along the windowsill. My first Thanksgiving that I was cooking. Straight date or not, I was gaying this shit up.

The next day, at the appointed time, the phone buzzed from the front desk and I went down to security to sign Jack in. He was carrying something rather large in his backpack. Nonetheless, security didn't care. I think the guard was mentally checked out as he barely looked at Jack's ID as I signed the clipboard on top of the desk.

"What's in the bag?" I questioned.

"A surprise for you. I think you're going to like it." I smiled nervously. We arrived at the 15th floor and I showed him into my dorm. "Very nice! For a dorm room," he said.

"Thanks. Yeah, I put my sewing skills to work to make it feel like less of a dorm."

"Oh, my God! Whatever you are making smells amazing!"

"Well, I was going to surprise you, but we are having bacon-wrapped roasted turkey, garlic mashed potatoes, cornbread stuffing, sautéed green beans, more cornbread on the side and pumpkin pie." He beamed.

"Thank you," he said, putting his hand on my shoulder, instantly turning me into a mushy pile. "So, you have a TV, right?"

"Of course," I said, pointing over in its direction.

"Great. I'm going to work on your surprise while you finish cooking."

"Deal," I said, heading off to the kitchen. I found myself humming one of his songs he played the night before. I knew zero would come of this evening, I understood its boundaries and yet I couldn't stop myself. I just wanted to spoil someone and to enjoy another man's company without all the bullshit that comes with dating gay men.

The turkey had been in the oven for quite some time. I slid the stuffing in the oven underneath it and began blanching the green beans. I opened a bottle of red wine and poured myself a glass. "You want a glass of wine?" I shouted from the kitchen.

"With dinner. You got a beer for now?" he said. I could tell he was doing something.

"Yes, but I don't want to ruin my surprise. It's in the fridge. Help yourself." He came in seconds later, grabbed his beer and left with a smile. God, I wish I could kiss him, I thought. Ugh, Kyle. Don't go down that road. It's a dead end, big time.

Everything for dinner was set. So was my surprise, which I could have after dinner. He asked if I had an extra sheet so he could cover the TV and my surprise. I thought this was odd, but directed him to my closet near the bathroom where I had one.

I left everything in the kitchen due to space constraints, and told him to grab his plate off the table and help himself. "Kyle, this is amazing. This looks and smells better than any Thanksgiving I've been to."

"I won't tell your mother," I said as he laughed and piled mashed potatoes onto his plate. After we had both filled our plates with Thanksgiving eats, we returned to the main room. I put his CD in my PowerBook and pressed play. He laughed at me, but didn't say to stop. We talked a lot during dinner. He said that he was from Jersey, grew up

Jewish, his parents were divorced and his sister was in L.A. trying to make it as a fashion designer to the stars. I spoke about growing up in Wisconsin and pursuing my dream of moving to New York to make it big. Just like the eight million other people.

"Seriously, Kyle, I don't know where you learned to cook like that. That was incredible."

"Well, two things: one there's still pumpkin pie, which I did not bake and two, I bought containers at the market so I am sending you home with half this food." His face looked like he had just seen a unicorn.

After we both had a slice of pie and I packed up his food, he said it was time for my surprise. I had wondered all throughout dinner what it could be. Then, he pulled two chairs in front of the TV, which had been shrouded in the sheet I lent him. He pulled it off with a "Ta da!"

Sitting in front of my TV was a black box and two controllers.

"Ok?" I said, drawing out my question.

"Not just ok. You will thank me later." He turned on the TV, handed me one of the controllers and started this magical black box sitting on my floor. "I give you: *Grand Theft Auto*!"

I had read about the game series in the news and dismissed it as adolescent and immature, never once stopping to actually check them out.

Jack started a new game and very passionately gave me the basic tour. I watched him as he stole cars, beat up hookers, went on missions to collect gambling debts. I was mesmerized by the level of detail in the game, from the soundtrack one could listen to in a stolen car, to the detail on the buildings and the people on the street. The inner 15 year old boy in me came out in full force and laughed at all the quirky and naughty nuances of the game.

Jack then handed the controller over to me and let me take a stab at it. I was immediately hooked. Like within ten-seconds hooked. I knew that after he left, I must go on amazon.com and order a game console and the latest copy of the game. No question.

We played for hours. I ducked out at one point to run to the bodega to get more beer to sneak back into the dorm. I was instantly obsessed with the game. Around 2AM, Jack started to yawn and decided it was time to take his leave. He unhooked the gaming system and I went into the kitchen to bag up his food. I didn't want him to go. I secretly wanted him to take a shower and crawl into bed with me. But, I knew that would never be in the cards for us. I shook the silliness off of me and realized that I had just made a great new friend, something I don't do easily and should be happy with that.

I loaded Jack up with his take out containers and he hugged me at the door. "Thank you, Jack. For keeping me company on this holiday and introducing me to the most amazing game ever."

"Thank you," he said. "For this amazing food and being a cool new friend." I patted his back and walked him down to security to sign him out. Ironic, if you think…the best date I've had in ages and it was with a straight guy.

Men with Ponytails

Barry was older than me by a good thirty years. I honestly have no reason why I agreed to meet him for coffee. I like to think that I was keeping an open mind. His photos looked good, he was employed, owned a townhouse in the Village, and was very charming during our chats. No apparent deterrents. And he was interested in me. That alone was an uphill battle.

I grabbed a Venti coffee and found a table at Starbucks. It was packed for a Saturday night. Who knew? Barry arrived a few minutes later. He was wearing a red plaid shirt, khakis and loafers with no socks. He had gold wireframe glasses, a neatly trimmed goatee and I could tell his hair was pulled back. As I stood to meet him, I saw that he had a full-on, down to his ass, pony tail. That wasn't in the pictures, I thought. Scratch that open-minded thing.

"Hi!" I said as he pulled me in to kiss my cheek.

"Hi, darlin'," he said with a Southern drawl. Wasn't expecting that either. "How are you?"

"I'm well. Can I get you anything?"

"No, you sit. I'll get a coffee." I took my seat as he headed off for the counter. Seriously? A ponytail? I had images running through my head of cutting it off as he slept.

He returned with his coffee. "It's so good to meet you!" he beamed again. I wish I felt the same.

"Likewise. Who knew that this was the happening Saturday night place?"

"Right?" he said, surveying the room.

"So. Tell me about the ponytail." I mean, why wait?

"Well," he chuckled. "I've grown my hair out since the 70's. I haven't had short hair since the 60's."

"Wow," I said. "That's commitment!" Well, it was.

"Yeah, sometimes I wear it up." Ok, that was worse, I thought. Turns out that Barry was big in the Studio 54 scene. Kinda made sense. Apparently, he was someone famous' houseboy. I could tell that Barry was ripped. I mean, for a guy pushing 60, he had a great body.

And a ponytail. Not sure if I was clear on that.

"So, you're a creative director. That's cool," I said, changing the subject away from his hair. "What kinds of projects are you working on?"

"Right now a national ad campaign for a sweater company." I thought of Sydney. "Do you want to take our coffee and walk around?" he asked.

"Sure," I said. Sounded harmless enough.

It was slightly muggy out and I instantly regretted not getting an iced coffee. We started walking down 8th avenue towards the Village. I assumed he was leading me back to his place. Turns out I was right.

"Do you want to come in?" he asked. "Just to see the place?" he assured.

"Ok," I said, walking up the steps to his townhouse. It was a very chic space. All the walls were a buttery cream color, the floors were honey oak and there were black accents everywhere. Most of his art and fixtures were very Deco. He had a giant zebra skin rug in his entryway. "I love your place!" I exclaimed. I did. It was very masculine, but felt very livable at the same time.

"Would you like anything to drink?" he asked from the kitchen. I was in the living room, inspecting his art.

"Campari would be great. If you have it."

"I do," he yelled. He entered the room with two glasses and stopped by a Bose stereo to turn it on. It was Erykah Badu. Not what I was expecting. He handed me my drink and I noticed he had a joint hanging from his mouth.

"You want?" he held it out to me.

"No, thanks." I stuck to liquor. My drug of choice. I never smoked a cigarette in my life, much less a joint. Oh, Barry. The cards are really stacked against you, I thought.

We stood awkwardly in his living room as I sipped my drink and he smoked his joint. I was feeling a little loopy from the contact high I was getting. I was at a loss for conversation and when he offered for us to watch old episodes of *Ab Fab*, I took him up on it.

A few drinks and episodes later, he started inching closer to me on the sofa. I tried to start a conversation or ask for another drink or got up to use the restroom to avoid his advances. When none of these things worked, I said I had to go.

"Really?" he said with obvious disappointment.

"Yeah, I should be going. Thank you for the drinks though!" He walked me to the front door, where we stood there for a few seconds without speaking.

"It's the ponytail, isn't it?" he blurted out.

"Yeah," I said, shook his hand and left. I saw Barry a couple of times for coffee and conversation. But yeah, it was the ponytail.

You're Not My Type #3

It was the weekend and Jim had gone home back upstate and Sydney was in North Carolina with her family. I had the place to myself. What do to? Maybe I'll make another attempt at finding some fun, I thought. Surely, there had to be a randy young man in a similar situation as myself.

I opened iTunes on my PowerBook and clicked play Miles Davis. I loved *Kind of Blue*. It was and remains my all-time favorite album. I pulled out my contraband wine and wineglass and poured that beautiful burgundy liquid. After chatting up a few guys online, I found one that I seemed to hit it off with. We agreed to meet. Not in a public place as I usually do, but at my apartment.

Quickly, I showered and slipped into a V-neck T-shirt and running shorts with no underwear. Easy access, I thought. And then I waited. Just me, Miles and pinot. I got lost in the music for a bit and a knock at the door startled me. "How did he get by security?" I thought. "Oh, God, was he a resident, too?"

"Hello," I said with a smile. There wasn't one on him. He was good-looking and well dressed. I kept waiting for him to greet me back, but it never came. His eyes swept over me, head to toe, and landed finally on my eyes. He shook his head from side to side and said "No." And bolted for the stairwell.

I closed the door, walked back to my desk and poured another glass of wine.

It's Fitting

Spring Break was finally upon us. The chill in the air had been lifted and the sun returned to the sky. Most of my friends had left the city to visit their families for the week and to celebrate Easter. I was one of the lone few who were left in the dorms. I was hoping Sydney would stay so we could get ourselves into some drunken trouble, but she was back in North Carolina, visiting her mom and dad.

It was Tuesday morning and I was restless. Usually, I am a homebody, happy to stay inside cooking, cleaning, playing video games, listening to music, chatting on the Internet. I didn't naturally crave human interaction. Today was another story.

I pulled on my jeans, Puma's, my favorite T-shirt advertising the old Atari game *Pitfall* and my trench coat and set out on the streets of New York. Again, something I never did. I started up towards Times Square and wandered east, winding over and up across the streets with no direction, no plan. I stopped and got a coffee from a deli and slowly sipped it and took in the people I passed, the snippets of conversations I overheard and the smells in the air. It was a rare, relaxed moment in the big city.

Soon, I was at Rockefeller Center. I stood above the dismantled ice skating rink and watched the water fall all around the Prometheus statue. I think I leaned against the railing for a good twenty minutes, enjoying my coffee. I never let myself do this, I thought and sighed. This was way better than any other Spring Break, I thought. I saw J.Crew across the way and decided to check out what was new. I tossed my empty cup in the bin and went in the store.

I loved everything about it - the chinos in fun colors, the brightly patterned ties, the perfectly sewn leather shoes, and the classic navy blazer. I had always preferred preppy clothes for myself. Anytime I dressed in something edgy, I just looked like I was trying too hard. I took a navy blue blazer off the rack and looked at the sewing details.

"It's beautiful, isn't it?" said a sweet, tender voice behind me.

"It is," I said, turning to see a beautiful Italian guy around my age with an innocent looking face and an intoxicating smile. I noticed Garbage's song "You Look So Fine" was playing above us.

"I'm Vinnie," he said, extending his hand.

"I'm Kyle," I said.

"I think that would look great on you," he said in a soft, flirty voice. I held it up in front of me and looked at it in the mirror. Everyone looks great in a navy blue blazer, I thought. "You want to try it on?" Before I could think, I nodded.

He led me across the store and towards the back where the dressing rooms were. He opened the door and set the blazer on the hook by the mirror. "Let me know if you need anything," he said, quickly looking at the floor after saying it. My knees started to get a little weak. Maybe it was the coffee on an empty stomach.

I closed the door and put the blazer on. It looked great. Two button front, side back vents, edge-stitching along the lapels, working button holes on the sleeves, lined in a bright orange color that made me smile. I wanted this blazer. I wanted Vinnie. The pulsating melody from Garbage was still playing above me. I closed my eyes and sighed.

When I opened my eyes, Vinnie was standing behind me. Normally, if I saw his reflection in the mirror, I would have jumped, but I smiled a slow smile as he approached me. He gently pulled the fabric at my waist and cinched it in.

"You have a great body. We would need to bring the sides in to make this more fitted." I smiled at him in the mirror. He took his fore fingers and rubbed them on either side of me where he had drawn the fabric in. He then leaned in and kissed me on the back of the neck and then another gentle kiss on the side. I was instantly hard.

Just then another sales associate was outside, directing a customer into the next booth. I looked at Vinnie and said: "I'll take it." We walked to the cash register, me trying to hide my hard-on. I handed the blazer across the counter and he took it from me with a smile. He rang it up. $595! In my haze of infatuation, I neglected to look at the price. No turning back now. I handed him my credit card and crossed my fingers it would go through. It did.

"Anything you want me to write on your receipt for you?" he asked coyly.

"Your number or email, perhaps?" I said. He scribbled down his number and email address on the back and handed it to me.

"Let's go out soon," he said.

"I'd like that." I grabbed my blazer and strolled out of the store, Garbage still pulsating in the background. I wanted to stay there with him. Perhaps clock in and help him. Or just spend the afternoon making out in the dressing room. I would have been fine with that.

I took my time walking home. I felt as though I were six inches off the sidewalk. I wandered up and down and over streets, not caring what direction I was going. Maybe he and I would hit it off and this would be the sexiest, most romantic story of how we met. We'd regale our friends over dinner and drinks about it, making them jealous and secretly aroused.

Back in my room, I hung the blazer in plain view. A trophy. I set the receipt on my desk and stared at his handwriting. It was reassuring to see someone else had serial killer handwriting. Often, I couldn't even read what I had written. But, I could spell out exactly what he had scribbled. Should I write him? Was that too desperate? I didn't exactly have any other men beating down my door and kissing me on the back of my neck.

I gave in and wrote him. I told him it was unbelievably romantic the way we met and I really wanted to take him out to dinner. I joked that I would make sure and wear my blazer. I clicked send. I sat back in my chair and breathed in a deep breath and felt good. This was so opposite from my normal experiences and here was something out of a story. That happened. To me.

All my friends were off enjoying their Spring Breaks and I couldn't get an immediate response from them about my story. I turned on the jazz station on the Internet radio and leaned back in my chair. I pulled the bottle of wine from my bottom desk drawer and glass and poured a little. I lit the candle next to my computer and sighed. Someone liked me! Me!

A few glasses later, my computer buzzed that I had a new email message waiting for me. It was from Vinnie. Immediately, my face went flushed and I was scared to open the message.

Kyle,

It was so great meeting you today. You are so cute. However, my ex just called me and really wants to give us another try. I feel like I have to. I'm sorry. But, you're great and you'll find someone for sure.

Vinnie

I deleted the email. The next day, I returned the blazer. To a different J.Crew.

Hey, Sailor!

Fleet Week is that very special time of year when the big warships park themselves in the New York Harbor and the beautiful, trim, white-clad men descend on our island. They flood the streets in search of drinking, sightseeing and of course, sex.

"My friend Timothy is on leave this week," said Sydney.

"Oh?" I said, flipping through a magazine at her kitchen table. Caryn was asleep on the floor, face planted on her *Betty Crocker* cookbook. I could make out that she had made her way up to the seafood section.

"He wants to meet up with us!"

"We have finals," I said, not looking up from *Vogue*.

"Finals will be over. It will be our celebration for making it through the year."

"Ok," I said closing the magazine. "Do you think she'll stay on the floor all summer?" I said, pointing to Caryn.

"Yeah, they'll probably wax the floor around her."

"You'll come back this fall and she'll still be here, face shellacked to that sea bass recipe." We laughed and I noticed drool rolling out of her mouth. Gross.

Pen down. My last final was complete. I breathed a sigh of relief. The school year was behind me. I grabbed my bag and left the classroom. Back in my room, I flopped down on my bed and closed my eyes. It was the perfect time for a nap. Except my phone buzzed on the table next to me.

> Sydney: We're on for tonight, right?
> Me: Yep.
> Sydney: Tavern?
> Me: Ok. I'll come to your room later.

The Tavern was this sketchy bar a few blocks from FIT. It was the anti-*Buon Gusto*. It was loaded with Fashion Merchandising girls and blue-collar workers. The merchandising girls, being surrounded by gay men all week, looked forward to flirting with straight men and having drinks bought for them. This was precisely why Sydney and I avoided this bar. I was curious why she chose it. Maybe Timothy had requested it. Maybe he wanted a merchandising girl for himself? Good luck with that, I thought.

Around 9 p.m., I knocked on Sydney's door.

"Hey, hey!" she said opening the door. I could tell she was pre-partying.

"Where's my drink?" I said, walking through the door.

"Kyle, this is Timothy," she said, proudly introducing the two of us. I shook his hand. He kind of looked just like the photo that Sydney had shared with me. Tall, lanky, boyish features and dressed in his sailor whites. Sydney handed me a drink. Caryn was still using her cookbook as a pillow.

"So, school's out for the summer!" he said, raising his drink.

"Yes, yes it is," I said sipping my drink. He was cute. This could be dangerous. Or fun. Or fun and dangerous. Sydney said he was "bi." That was good enough for me. 50/50 odds were better than nothing.

We finished our drinks and started the walk up to *The Tavern*. It was dark and nasty and smelled like stale beer and the floor always crunched beneath your feet. I couldn't ever make out what exactly was crunching and figured it was best to leave that one a mystery. We found a booth way in the back and Timothy said he would order us drinks. He put his hand on my arm and I felt a surge of electricity run through me.

"What are you drinking, Kyle?" he asked.

"Vodka on the rocks," I said, guessing they had no Campari.

"Isn't he cute?" Sydney asked after he was out of range.

"Very," I said. But, I couldn't tell if it was him or the uniform I was smitten with. I never fancied myself the type to go for any man in uniform, but there was something about a sailor's outfit that got me. "Why don't the two of you hook up?" I asked.

"I wanted to, but he never did. Which makes me believe that he likes your team better than mine." That would be a first. I laughed.

Timothy set our drinks on the table and we thanked him for them. He sat down next to me. I could feel his leg touching mine. Again, a jolt of electricity raced through my body. I put my hand on my leg and seconds later, I could feel his hand touching mine. Not locking fingers, but they were touching and neither of us moved.

We spoke about summer plans, where Timothy had sailed and how we were dreading the fall semester. The drinks kept coming. And coming. And coming. Timothy always managed to be touching me under the table. I felt so alive. The semester was done, a cute sailor was sitting next to me, quietly and unassumingly touching me and alcohol pumping through my body. It was magical.

I've got to go home, I thought, suddenly recognizing that I had consumed way too much vodka. I took my leave and stumbled the three blocks back to FIT. I didn't remember making the schlep, just arriving in my dorm room, running for the bathroom where I had dry heaves in the sink. Jim was there, asking me if I was ok. I assured him I was ok and tucked myself into bed.

I woke the next day to the worst hangover on record. Even turning my head an inch set off waves and pangs of pain. I told Jim to take money from my wallet and get me Taco Bell and a giant Diet Dr. Pepper. It wasn't until around 7 p.m. that night I was actually able to get out of bed. A shower helped immensely. After getting dressed, I stumbled down the hall to Sydney's.

"You look like shit," she said, opening the door.

"Thank you. I feel like it." I sat down at her table. Caryn had rolled over, creating a crease on the page. Sydney poured me a cup of coffee. She, too, was nursing a hangover by the looks of it. "How much did I drink last night?"

"No idea, but man, you were wasted."

"Really? I didn't think it was that bad. I remember saying good-bye to you guys and stumbling back to the dorms." She let out a chuckle. "What?" I said.

"Here," she said, turning her laptop towards me. "Want to see pictures?"

Pictures? Oh, dear Lord. Up on the screen was a photo of me, shirtless, up in Timothy's arms with a band of merchandising girls raising their glasses to us. The next one was me with his sailor's hat on and a look on my face like I had no idea where I was and didn't care. The following one featured me standing on the bar, still shirtless, swinging my shirt and trying to make a sexy, squatted pose. The next was Timothy and I completely lip-locked. The following was me slouched down in our booth with Sydney drawing on my chest with a Sharpie. The next was two merchandising girls playing tic-tac-toe on my chest with Sydney's Sharpie while I sat eyes closed, with a huge grin. The next was me standing behind Timothy, kissing his neck and unbuttoning his uniform. The last was myself and the tic-tac-toe girls kissing his chest.

"I don't remember any of this," I said, embarrassed.

"You were epic." I pulled up my shirt to reveal the tic-tac-toe game (X's won) and Sydney's drawings.

"Oh, my God, it actually happened."

"Yup!" she said with pride that I didn't just come out of my shell, but ran out and kicked it as far away from me as possible.

"Did Timothy and I sleep together?" I asked with hesitation.

"No."

"Damn."

Glitter Boy

I'm a procrastinator. I admit it. Openly, freely and willingly. I do my best work under pressure. So, of course, I leave everything to the last possible minute. My final garment for our student runway show was no exception.

I took a swig from a 40 and pinned some muslin haphazardly to the dress form. Sydney was intensely working next to me, infinitely farther along than me.

"Um, aren't you concerned about being cut from the show?" she asked, looking at me with concern, and taking a drink of her beer. We always snuck beer into the draping lab. Tonight's selection was Colt 45.

"I'll get it done. Always do," I said, really trying to convince both of us.

"It's in two days!"

"I know," I said. I took out my sketchbook and flipped through it. Nothing was speaking to me. I usually had more than enough ideas, but I was really at a loss. Sydney was a Knitwear major and she was making this gorgeous knit dress with a giant cowl and these amazing cuffs that weren't attached to the dress itself. It was all very space age but chic at the same time. What was I going to do? This was my only last design statement of my college education. I had to make it count.

Just then, Glitter Boy walked past the draping lab. "That's him!" I exclaimed and nudged Sydney to look at the door. I had a crush on Glitter Boy since the first day of college. He was a couple of people ahead of me in the orientation line. He was shorter than me, adorable face, curly brown hair, deep brown eyes, pale skin and had a gentle, unassuming nature about him. My heart melted every time I saw him. Which was often. We had a knack of running into one another at least once a week, over the course of four years.

"*That's* him?" Sydney said, almost dropping her beer bottle on the floor, not watching where she was setting it.

"He's adorable!" I defended my crush on him. And his nickname. Ok. So, I was coming back to the dorms late one night from across the street in the draping lab and I saw him coming out of the elevator. I did a double take. His entire face was covered in glitter paint. He was wearing a skin-tight white tank top and the shortest shorts I had ever seen. His arms and neck were painted with glitter, even his legs were painted with glitter. He smiled and winked at me as he got off the elevator as I was getting on. We had several exchanges like this. I could only imagine where he was headed dressed like that, but I still found him adorable. I just blocked the glitter part out, but the name stuck.

"I'm going after him!" I said, throwing caution to the wind, and my muslin. Out in the hall, I could see that he was headed to the "A" Building, probably going to dinner. I rushed to catch up with him and then played it cool, not trying to make it so obvious I was there to see him.

He turned and saw me and flashed his usual toothy smile. "Hi," he said. He had a great voice. It dawned on me that it was the first time I had ever heard it.

"Hi," I said. "How are you?"

"Good! I was just going to grab something to eat. What about you?"

"Oh, I am working on my term garment. Well, I'm watching my friend work on hers while I drag my feet."

"Selection is in two days!" Why was everyone on me? I would get it done! We made small talk for a while and then made plans for him to come over to my room the following night. Jim would be gone, I thought, so I would have him all to myself. He was coming over under the guise of helping me with my garment.

"I have a date!" I said proudly as I returned to Sydney.

"With a dress form and a sewing machine," she said, pins in her mouth.

"No! With Glitter Boy!"

"He better be helping you sew." I sighed and sat back on my stool. Finally inspiration hit. Maybe it was the prospect of getting laid that got the creative juices flowing, but suddenly I had a vision of doing a quilted and beaded cape in a deep wine color to go with the mauve strapless jumpsuit with a plaid pattern sewn on top of out of cashmere yarns. Sydney nodded and said "Me likey." I quickly busted out the patterns for both and finished my beer.

The next morning I went fabric shopping. I could have spent the afternoon cutting out the pieces, but instead I napped. When I woke, I lined the windowsill with tea-lights in my favorite little clear glass votives, shut off all the lights except the lamp next to my bed, put Count Basie on in iTunes. I ran to the bathroom and brushed my teeth and sprayed on Dolce & Gabbana cologne.

The knock came promptly at 10. "Hey you," I said, opening the door. He was so hot. And thankfully, not covered in glitter. I'd never get that shit out of my sheets, I thought.

I showed him in to the room. "Wow! You decorated. This is great," he said looking at the framed art and throw pillows that I had put together. I offered him a glass of wine and he accepted. "Cheers!" he said, clinking his glass to mine. We took sips from our glasses and he noticed the drawings on the table. "Is this your final design?"

"Yes!" I said with excitement. "I am doing this jumpsuit with this cape. It's all about surface texture. Creating pattern on top of the garment instead of weaving it into or printing on the fabric."

"I love it," he said inching in closer to me.

"These are the fabrics that I'm using." I showed him the mauve silk crepe and the wine satin. His hand met mine on top of the swatches and we immediately turned, faced one another and kissed. We stood there for several minutes, kissing and holding one another.

He pulled me over to my bed and I fell back, with him landing on top of me. We continued kissing has he unbuttoned my dress shirt and pants. I pulled off his T-shirt and played with his chest hair. He had the sexiest chest in the world. I unbuttoned his pants and he finished pulling them off. Our naked bodies now touching, we continued to kiss as I caressed his back. Soon, the deal was sealed.

Getting dressed, I went into full-on panic mode. I pressed my muslin patterns, laid out the fabric, cut the pieces, basted them together, and started sewing the major seams. Glitter Boy, having brought his own sewing machine, constructed the cape. By 11:30 p.m., the only thing that was left, was the plaid pattern and the quilting and beading. All the handwork. The hard stuff.

"Sydney," I said frantically on the phone. "Can you please come over and help me sew? I'm never going to finish." Reluctantly, she agreed. Jim was with her. He had already finished his Graphic Design final so he was free too. I wondered for a second, why he was at her place, but didn't care. I needed as many hands as possible.

I made quick introductions between Sydney, Jim and Glitter Boy and promptly showed Jim how to sew beads on the cape.

"You have Jim sewing? You must be desperate," Sydney said as she started unwinding the cashmere yarns for the plaid pattern. The four of us sewed and sewed and sewed. For hours we didn't speak, completely focused on the handwork in front of us.

Finally, around 5 a.m., Glitter Boy said he had to leave. He still had a few finishing touches on his garment that he needed to sew. I walked him to the door and kissed him goodbye.

Back at the worktable, Sydney blurted out: "So? How was Glitter Boy?"

"Huh?" Jim said, not taking his eyes off his beading.

"Are you ready for this?" I didn't wait for an answer. "Worst. Sex. Ever."

"What?" they both said in unison, looking up at me.

"He just laid there! I thought given his playful nature, he would have been a force in bed. It was the biggest disappointment."

Maybe I had built it up too much in my mind. Weeks, months and years pining for him and fantasizing about him only set me up for failure.

Around 9 a.m., we finished. I thanked them for their work, made a pot of coffee and texted my model to meet me at the auditorium for our 10 a.m. garment selection review. Turned out, my creation won the tailored garment award and would be the highlight of the show. Another one pulled out of my ass.

I didn't see Glitter Boy again until four years later, when I ran into him at Whole Foods, buying artichokes.

Porn Star

Graduation was upon us. It was kind of bittersweet. I was ready to be done with tests and projects and the like, but I wasn't looking forward to not having Sydney down the hall from me. What was I going to do? She and I avoided the subject at all costs. Denial was best. I had already said goodbye to Jim, who moved back upstate to be with his girlfriend.

"Dude," Jack said over drinks at *Buon Gusto*, after his set. "There's an apartment open in my building. We should be neighbors!" Initially, I dismissed the idea. I wasn't sure I wanted him knowing my comings and goings and I his. But, I wasn't having much luck on my own finding a place and Jack and I could hang out and play *Grand Theft Auto* together. I made an appointment and met Jack and the landlord there.

I was delightfully surprised. Jack neglected to inform me that the one bedroom apartment had been recently remodeled. Everything in it was brand new. I touched the shiny new appliances in the kitchen and pictured myself cooking there, sitting at the table, enjoying coffee. "I'll take it!" I exclaimed, not masking my enthusiasm at all.

The transaction happened at lightning speed. I put the deposit down, paid the first month's rent and signed the lease. Done. Now I just needed to graduate and move out of the dorms. Things seemed to be on track. If only Sydney could rent an apartment in the building and we would be a sitcom. She had chosen to live out in Brooklyn. The world dropped off on either side of Manhattan for me. It wasn't that I was a zip code snob, I just liked what I was used to.

Back in my dorm room, I threw some clothes into a moving box and sat down on the edge of my bed. I should have one last hurrah in my dorm room, I thought. I went to my computer and scanned the personal ads. I stopped at a picture of a hot guy wearing nothing, but a blue Speedo. When I wasn't looking at his washboard abs, I was looking at the package beneath that Speedo. His name was Michael Blu. An odd last name, but I went with it. At least his name and his speedo coordinated. These details are important.

He wrote me back. I was shocked. We agreed he would come over, one last romp in the dorms. The front desk buzzed that he was there and I quickly ran down to meet him. He had glasses on that he didn't in his photo and made him look older for some reason. He was still striking. We made pleasantries as I signed him in. In the elevator we didn't talk much. I was wondering if he was going to tell me I was not his type and leave. Which would be really awkward as I would have to sign him back out.

In my room, I offered him a drink. He declined. "No, I need to be good for tomorrow for work."

"Oh? What is it that you do?" Finally. Conversation.

"Umm," he hesitated. "I'm in film."

"Like an actor? Have I seen you in anything?"

"Possibly," he hesitated again. I stood, staring at him for him to elaborate. "I'm in porn."

"Wow! I've never met a real live porn star!" It was like witnessing a wild animal out of his natural habitat. I thought of Jimmy and the adult video store.

"In fact, I'm filming tomorrow." My interest was piqued. He was telling me the plotline for the film. He was the repair guy who shows up to fix a phone line or window or something at a hot guy's house and things get steamy.

"So, this is practice for tomorrow?" I asked coyly.

"Kinda, but I can't go all the way."

"What do you mean?" I said confused. I thought I was going to get the royal porn star experience.

"I need to, um, save it for the movie."

"Ah," I said with a disappointed look on my face.

"Don't worry though! This can be all about you." Not a bad prospect, but still! When was I going to have a real live porn star in my bed again? "Come here," he said, pulling me close and kissing me. The kisses were just ok. Again, I was looking to be blown away.

We flopped down on my bed with him landing on top of me. I could feel his gigantic penis getting hard in between us. He took off my shirt and gently kissed my chest. I took off his shirt, exposing that perfect abdomen. I touched it in disbelief, my fingers falling in and out of the muscle lines. I couldn't fathom the amount of work that took.

He unbuttoned my chinos and slid them off, along with my boxers. There I was, naked, in all my not chiseled glory for him to view. I thought he would get up and run, but he didn't. He was about to take me in his mouth when we heard the key go in the lock. Jim! Damnit! He was supposed to be out for the evening. We both grabbed our clothes and ran for the bathroom.

"Shit!" he said.

"What?"

"I forgot my underwear out there." We stood silently, listening to see if Jim was just collecting something and leaving. Maybe he would see the underwear on the floor and put two and two together. I heard the famous Apple chime, indicating that he started his computer. He was there to stay.

"Well, let's make the most of this," he said, getting on his knees and started to give the worst blowjob in the history of sex. It felt as though the tips of his teeth were scraping of a layer of skin with every motion. I pulled him off of me and finished myself. If you want something done right, sometimes you just have to do it yourself. I cleaned up and got dressed. I felt guilty for not taking care of him, but at the same time, the sex was so bad, I was just glad it was over.

I pressed my ear to the door to hear if Jim at left yet. Sounded like he did. I ran out and grabbed Michael's underwear and tossed them into the bathroom. He cleaned up and came out. He gave me a hug. Even that felt awkward and unnatural. I walked him down to the front desk and signed him out.

The next day he wrote me:

Hey! Shoot was canceled. Going to be next week. Want to finish what we started?

Nah, I said. I was good.

Made-To-Measure

"Welcome aboard," said Dick, my new boss at the venerable old tailoring firm, *Books Brothers* (as we will call it here). My first job after college.

"Thank you," I said, shaking his hand.

"Let's get you to your desk," he said with a smile. He was a large and imposing guy, prematurely balding and had a salt and pepper goatee, but there was something magnetic about him at the same time. I was thrilled to have landed the job as assistant in the made-to-measure department. I loved the idea of one-of-a-kind garments being hand-sewn to someone's specific measurements. It was my job to work with the sales associates and the factories to make sure everything went smoothly. "Here you go," he said, presenting the cubicle to me.

"Great," I said, setting my bag down on the desk. It was easily double the size of my internship cube and I could see sunlight coming through the door of an open office. This was a definite step in the right direction. Until I could get my own shiny office, that is.

Over the next six months, I settled into my role famously. I had developed a great rapport the sales associates and factories alike. Dick pretty much left me to manage my time and workload. It was a great place to be at.

"I have a very special project for you," said Dick.

"What is that?" I asked enthusiastically.

"I need you to take these suits over to Wynton." And by Wynton, he meant Marsalis. Our company outfitted *Jazz at Lincoln Center*. This was a task that Dick usually kept for himself.

Suits in hand, I rounded up our best tailor and hailed a cab. At the Time Warner Center, we were met by Wynton's assistant, Vicki. "Have you been here before?" she asked us. We shook our heads. "Come on!" she said proudly, offering us on a private tour of the many performance spaces, event hall, educational spaces. Being a huge jazz fan, it was a rare experience and I was beside myself with glee.

"Let's go see Wynton," she said. We were shown into his dressing room. A comfortable, windowless room that had a sofa, a chair and a baby grand piano. The tailor, Alfredo, and I sat on the sofa waiting Wynton's arrival.

"Gentlemen!" he said with a huge smile as he entered the dressing room. He was shorter than I expected, but he exuded charm and grace. We shook his hands and he handed me his trumpet, "Here, would you mind setting this down for me?" he asked, taking off his suit jacket and Alfredo putting a new one on him. I looked down at the trumpet in my hands. Oh, my God, I thought to myself, this is the instrument of legendary performances and recordings. Wow. I gently set it down on the sofa.

I returned several times over the next year to deliver custom shirts and suits to Wynton. He always met me with a smile and a pat on the shoulder. He never did learn my name, though. He just called me Mr. Books.

Every day I made my rounds. Our offices were located above our flagship location. I started my day by visiting each of the floor managers, exchanging pleasantries and checking to see if there were any issues I could support them with. I ended my rounds on the ground floor – custom shirts and ties.

"Hello, Terri." I said shaking her hand. "How are you?"

"Look who's at my desk!" she said with excitement. I saw a distinguished looking old man sitting there, waiting patiently for her to return.

"Is that Walter Cronkite?" I asked. She nodded like a schoolgirl. "My friend is a reporter. She went to journalism school because of him. Can I meet him?" She motioned to follow.

"Mr. Cronkite, this is Kyle Meyers, our fabulous custom order assistant."

"Pleasure to meet you," he said, his voice unmistakably his.

"I don't normally do this, but could I trouble you for your autograph? My friend went to journalism school because of you. You are her hero." He smiled a smile and looked down. I could only suspect that he was thinking back to the span of his career and all of the people he influenced.

"Of course," he said with a smile. I picked up a pad and a pen and handed it to him. "What's her name?"

"Lisa," I said. He scribbled on the notepad and handed it back to me.

"Tell Lisa, thank you." I said I would and thanked him and left him to be fitted for his shirts. I looked down on the pad and he had written: "Lisa, thank you. The world needs you more than ever. Walter Cronkite." I framed it and gave it to her that year for Christmas.

Once, I was sitting at my desk, flipping through fabric swatches when the phone rang. It was Louisa, an incredibly sweet elderly lady who worked at one of our Chicago stores.

"Kyle? I have someone to who would like to speak with you."

"Put them on!" I said. I liked her. I had helped her rush through several orders successfully.

"Kyle?" inquired a very familiar voice. "I want to thank you for getting me my tuxedo in time for the Oscars." It was Roger Ebert. He had recently lost weight and was in need of a new tuxedo. I, of course, helped out.

"You are very welcome, sir." I responded. These were definitely the memories I was going to take with me.

You're Not My Type #4

It had been forever since I was laid. I admit it freely. And it needed to happen. Now. I met Mark on-line, exchanged photos and agreed to hookup. He said he was working as an assistant or something at the Broadway show, *The Producers*. He said there was a storage room there that we could have fun in. The idea intrigued me, so I agreed.

Stepping out of the shower, I thought, I hope I don't smell. It was summer and I usually take three showers at a minimum. I put deodorant on, brushed my teeth and sprayed myself with Armani cologne. Hopefully, I wouldn't sweat much before meeting. After, didn't matter, I thought. I would walk home in the afterglow of both of our sweat mixed together. I sighed.

I set out for Times Square. It was brutal out, pushing 98 degrees and humid. I could feel sweat forming in the small of my lower back. I got there early, as I always do. I stood next to the service entrance as instructed. I was wearing jeans and a navy V-neck T-shirt and red sneakers. I told Mark this so I would be easily recognized. I wasn't wearing any underwear. That was my little surprise for him.

I watched the tourists shuffle past me, looking lost and frazzled, carrying souvenirs and pamphlets and menus collected from people passing them out on the corners. No New Yorker ever accepts those. An elderly couple stopped and asked me if they were headed east or west. "West," I said, pointing them in the right direction. You can take me out of Wisconsin, but you can't take the Wisconsin out of me, I thought and smiled, knowing I guided them in the right direction.

It seemed to be nearing the designated meeting time. I checked my phone. Five minutes past. He probably had some last minute costume or set crisis and that's why Mark hadn't opened the service door. Several people had come and gone, I studied each of them, but none looked like his photo. I'll give it another five minutes and then I'll text him, I thought. Beads of sweat now dotted my hairline.

"Do you know a good restaurant around here?" a young British couple asked me. I told them about a little Thai place I knew in Hell's Kitchen that I adored. The Pad Thai was the best in the city, I told them. They thanked me profusely. I really just wanted them to leave, what if they were scaring Mark off by chatting me up?

I checked my phone. Fifteen minutes past. I decided to text him.

Me: Hey! Where are you? I'm here.

After about five more minutes, I finally got a response.

Mark: Sorry. Not my type.

I shut my phone off and started walking down 7th avenue towards my apartment. I stopped and got a Jamba Juice. Blueberry pomegranate. I kind of zoned out, brain freeze from the frozen juice. Am I anyone's type? I asked myself.

Matchy, Matchy

Nicholas met me at a 24-hour diner on 6th avenue for brunch on Sunday. I stood nervously outside, waiting for him to arrive. We began chatting online for a week and decided it was time to meet face-to-face. He was the most promising lead I had in a long time. He was an aspiring screenwriter, having just moved back from L.A., to make a go of it in New York. His parents lived in Jersey City, so he was staying with them until he found his own place.

During our chats, he spoke about this book that he really wanted to read, called *Never Coming To A Theater Near You*, a book about unsung cinema hits. I had it neatly wrapped in the craft bag I was holding. I watched the people that passed, looking for his face to emerge on a stranger.

There he was. I recognized him instantly. Dark brown, receding hair, trimmed beard and the most adorable brown eyes. He was a little bit taller than me and had a slight belly. He was perfect.

"Hi!" I said, extending my hand.

"What's this handshaking thing? C'mere!" he said and pulled me in for a hug. I was immediately drawn to him. "You hungry?"

"I can always eat," I said.

"Good! Let's eat."

We were seated at a booth in the back, away from the bustle of the cash register area and the lunch counter. I kept stealing glances at him across my menu, each time to find him glancing back at me, smiling. I ordered my standby: scrambled eggs, bacon, toast, home fries and black coffee. Nicholas ordered an egg white omelet with sautéed spinach and mushrooms. Maybe it was an L.A. thing. I felt guilty for a nanosecond and focused back on him.

"Oh! I have something for you," I announced, handing him the gift. He accepted it with a smile. Carefully, he unwrapped each side, although it was painfully obvious it was a book of some kind.

"Oh, my God! You are the absolute sweetest person! You were listening to me!" he said, carefully opening the cover and glancing at a few pages.

"You spoke so highly of this book that I wanted you to have a copy."

"Thank you," he beamed and our feet found one another under the table and he squeezed my leg with his. He continued to leaf through the book as I sipped my coffee. This is the perfect Sunday, I thought. Here I am, at a diner with a hot guy, he's flipping through a book and I haven't a care in the world. I wish this moment could last forever.

"What are you currently listening to on your iPod?" he asked.

"Huh?" I said, confused.

"You can tell everything about a person based on their iPod library." I let out a laugh. "C'mon! Let's exchange." With that, I pulled my iPod out of my bag and placed it in his hands took his in return. He listened to a great deal of

Pulp, Smiths, Radiohead, The Cure, Depeche Mode. Pretty much what I had expected.

"You seriously listen to Tom Jones?" he asked, holding my iPod back at me as proof.

"Ok, I think this game is over," I said and he busted out laughing, pulling my iPod from his hand.

Over the next hour, we leisurely ate our food and chatted. Everything about being with him was completely natural. After splitting the check, we decided to wander around the area. Heading east on 15th street, he quietly took his hand in mine. I was beaming. We wandered into West Elm and pointed out the furniture that we both liked. It felt like a very 'couples' thing to do on a New York Sunday.

Close to dinnertime, I walked him to the Path train, to go to his parents' house in Jersey. I didn't want to leave him. I wanted to take him back to my place and watch one of the movies in the book I had given him. We stood for a while and finally he leaned in and kissed my cheek. I watched him walk down the stairs into the station. He stopped just before he was out of view and waved at me. I waved back.

I chose not to take the train back to my apartment, but instead, walked the twenty blocks. I felt like I levitated the whole way home. *Finally!* Finally, I had met someone that I was attracted to, clicked with and he found me attractive as well.

Over the next few weeks, we wrote to one another on and off throughout the day and saw each other several times. We were always on-point with one another: the proverbial finishing each other's sentences, one meeting we both showed up with mix CDs we made for the other, always were craving the same foods at mealtime, and even began having inside jokes. Our courtship was slow and quiet and romantic. My soul had been begging for this and here it was, in front of me.

"You really like this guy!" Jack exclaimed as he stole a car in *Grand Theft Auto*.

"Yeah, I really do."

"Dude, don't fuck it up." I shot him a look, which he didn't see, engrossed in the game.

"How's your love life?" I changed the subject.

"You know me. I do alright." I could only imagine what that meant. "When are you seeing him again?"

"Tonight. He's coming over."

"Spending the night?" he asked, teasing me. My face was bright red.

"Yes." He paused the game.

"Ooooooooonh!" he wailed.

"Stop it! Play your game."

"Don't fuck it up," he repeated.

I really wanted to the evening to be special. I got fresh cut flowers from the bodega on the corner and was preparing my famous chicken potpie. Nicholas said he would bring the wine. I went on iTunes and created a "Nicholas Date

Playlist" full of romantic jazz standards and classic love songs. Tea-lights were flickering on every surface.

The buzzer rang and I let Nicholas in. "Hey you," I said as I opened the door. He was so beautiful. Not conventionally so, but there was something about him that was irresistible to me. He handed me a bouquet of roses and leaned in and then stopped.

"Can I kiss you?" We hadn't kissed until that moment!

"Yes, of course." And then it happened. It was perfect. Now I was really excited for later.

"That was nice," he said, opening his eyes again.

"Come in," I offered. He set his overnight bag down by the door and looked around.

"Wow. This place is incredible. You should be an interior designer."

"Yeah, it's a hobby of mine." He walked around, inspecting the photos that lined the wall behind the sofa. I had framed close to 30 photographs of people I admired, respected or loved. I wanted them looking over me, guiding me.

"This is so cool," he said turning from the wall to flash me one of those heart-melting smiles.

"Yeah, I liked the idea of being surrounded by images of people I admire."

"What is that smell?" he said, getting a whiff of the pastry turning golden in the oven.

"Chicken potpie."

"Amazing. Oh, that reminds me, here's the wine." He pulled out a bottle. It looked fancy. At least fancier than the wines my bodega sold.

"I'll open it and let it breathe." I took the bottle from him and walked over to the kitchen area and got the corkscrew out. "Thank you for bringing wine. That was really sweet of you."

"It was very sweet of you to make me dinner," he said, coming up behind me and kissing me on the back of my neck. Chills swept over my body and I was instantly hard. Tonight is going to be phenomenal, I thought.

"No problem," I said, turning around, trying to hide my erection. We kissed again and he squeezed my shoulders together.

"So cute," he said as he walked back to the living room area.

"Really?" I said and immediately regretted it.

"You are very cute."

"It's just not something I hear very often." I blushed.

"Well, it's the truth. And you'll be hearing a lot more of it." I liked the sound of that.

I checked on the potpie. Almost done. I poured Nicholas a glass of wine and took it to him. He was now seated on my sofa, looking at the giant Marc Rothko print hanging above my television.

"You really do have a beautiful apartment." I handed him his wine.

"Thank you. I've always felt like home should be this oasis you get to return to after battling the city and eight million people every day."

"I like that." Somehow, I thought he was cataloging these moments for his screenplay. Even so, I didn't mind. They were magical and they were mine. I took the potpie out of the oven and sat it on the table in between where we would sit. I tossed a simple mesclun salad and set the serving utensils next to the pie.

"Come," I said waving him over. "Let's eat."

Nicholas sat his wine down next to his plate. "This looks fantastic! You have no idea how much this means to me that you took the time to cook!" I had a flash memory of making it in the dorms and leaving the carcass for Sydney. I smiled.

"You are very welcome. Any time."

"I am going to take you up on that," he said.

"Well, let's see how your first meal goes!" We laughed and I offered him the utensils to help himself to as much as he wanted. He took a good-sized portion, which came as a relief. I took an equally big portion.

"This is delicious!" he exclaimed after the first bite.

"Thank you!" I started to eat as well. For the next hour or so we feasted, even helping ourselves to seconds and plenty of wine. We spoke about the upcoming Presidential election and how mortified we were about the thought of a second term for Bush. Aligned on politics. Check. He regaled me with a few tales of life in L.A., the celebrities he met and the funny encounters he had with them. I asked him about his time at the big studios as a writer. His legs wrapped around mine under the table, just as they had at our first meeting.

After dinner, I told him to make himself comfortable on the sofa and I would wrap up the leftovers and load the dishwasher. He flopped back, wine in hand and I cleaned. I would love to cook and clean for him every night, I thought. I poured myself another glass of wine (we were on bottle two by now) and joined him on the sofa.

"What do you want to watch?" I asked.

"What do you have?"

"There's that stack of DVDs in the basket under the TV and there's two Netflix discs next to it." He got up and scanned my offerings.

"Let's watch *Happiness*," he said.

"Excellent choice," I said, getting up to put the disc in and turn the TV on.

"Come here," he said, taking my hand and leading me to sit so I was leaning back on his chest. He smelled so good. I remember thinking, this is one of the most romantic things I've ever experienced. We watched the movie and despite my having seen it a thousand times, I don't remember watching any of it. I closed my eyes and for two hours, I let myself be held and received the occasional kiss on the top of my head.

"Oh! I have something for you!" I exclaimed after the movie, remembering the surprise I bought him. I ducked into the bedroom and pulled out a beautiful, shiny navy box with the *Books Brothers* golden emblem embossed on the surface.

"Kyle, you didn't have to get me anything!"

"Nonsense. I get a discount and I wanted you to have something nice." I handed him the box.

"What is this?" he said taking the lid off. Inside was a pair of beautiful sateen navy pinstripe pajama top and bottoms. "I've never owned a pajama set like this. This may very well be the nicest piece of clothing I own." I was full of pride.

"Go put them on!" I said. He stood up, kissed me and took them into the bathroom. While he was in there, I had what I thought was a great idea. I went in the bedroom and slipped into the very same, matching pajamas. I stood in the living room and waited for him to come out.

"This fabric is so ni…" he said coming out of the bathroom, stopping dead in his tracks when he saw me. "Umm," he said, shoulders dropped.

"I have a set, too!" I said joyfully.

"So, I see." He stood there motionless for what seemed like an hour. "Ok. This is too weird."

"What do you mean?" I asked, completely dumbfounded. What had happened?

"I've got to go," he said, grabbing his overnight bag and left. Still in his new *Books Brothers* pajamas.

I sat down on the sofa and started to cry. That was the last time I ever wore those pajamas.

High-Wire Act

The bulk of my work at *Books Brothers* was to support the stores with their custom orders. If it meant rushing a tuxedo order through for a gentleman's wedding, a suit for a shareholder meeting or a shirt and tie for a job interview, I made it happen. I used my charm and Midwestern upbringing to get the factories and fabric suppliers on my side. I had close relationships established with each. I sent holiday cards, remembered their family members' birthdays and inquired about details mentioned during previous chats.

I had garnered the reputation that I could make things happened. And I did. I also developed relationships with the sales associates around the country, who called me frantically for help. Many of them I never met, but would know their voices anywhere. One of them was a guy by the name of David. He worked in the Wall Street store. I could tell he was gay, but I knew nothing about him. Maybe he was happily partnered. Who knew?

"Kyle!" he said in the tone I knew all too well, which meant: I'm in a crisis and you must solve it for me.

"David!" I said recognizing his voice. I pictured him six feet tall, dark brown hair, crystal blue eyes, chiseled like a guy in a shaving cream commercial. "How can I help?"

"I'm screwed." My mind went to a naughty place.

"What's the issue?" I said, pulling up my email.

"I completely forgot to place an order for a client. A suit for his son's graduation from Yale," he said, his voice shaken.

"How bad are we talking?" I asked.

"Next week is the fitting." He was screwed. The average lead-time was four weeks. I've been known to work magic, but this was going be like a sermon on the mount.

"Email me the order details." I waited while he sent me the measurements and fabric details. I could hear him breathing on the phone. I had secretly wondered what he looked like. I thought of showing up at the store and pretending to be a customer, just to get to meet him. "Ok, I have it in front of me," I said. I scanned it quickly. It was with the factory in Brooklyn. That was a plus. Margie, my counterpart there, adored me. "Let me make a call. I'll call you right back," I said.

"Thank you! Thank you!" he gushed.

"You can thank me after I fix this." I hung up the phone. I know how you can thank me, I thought. "Margie, I've got a good one for you..." I said and recounted the situation to her. She also knew of my crush on David, so that made her eager to help me out. She made a few calls to their production floor and twenty minutes later, I had confirmation the suit would be done in four days. A new record for me.

"David?" I said, calling him back.

"Yes?" he said with anticipation.

"You owe me big time. The suit will be ready in four days."

"Oh, my God! Are you serious?"

"Yup. This is my personal best record. I'm quite proud of myself, actually."

"Oh, my God, I do owe you." I laughed, taking a sip from my coffee, basking in my professional achievement.

Four days later, I arranged for the custom suit to be messengered to the Wall Street store. David emailed me confirmation that he received it, the fitting went well (just hemming on the trousers and minor adjustments to the sleeves) and the customer would have the suit in time for the commencement ceremonies.

"You are the absolute best, Kyle. You really are."

"Tell Dick that," I said.

"I already wrote him an email."

"That was really sweet of you." I blushed.

"I don't know how much good it will do." He knew about Dick. Everyone did. Dick had turned into a monster. I choked back a laugh.

"True."

"Listen, I don't want to sound presumptuous, but would you like to have dinner with me? I've been meaning to ask you out and now I have to thank you for your help."

"I'd love to," I said like a schoolgirl, my face completely flush.

"Oh, that's a relief. I was so nervous you'd say no! I've had a crush on you since you started and I've been dying to meet you!"

"It's funny you say, that, I've felt the same about you!"

"Perfect," he said in the sweetest voice. I was melting. "When are you free?"

"Well, you know my schedule."

"True." He laughed. "How about Thursday? I have trapeze class, but we could meet after!"

"What class?" I said, stunned.

"Trapeze. I had always wanted to do it so a few years ago. So, I started and have been hooked ever since!" Instantly, I thought of circus performers with their trim bodies and their skintight costumes. He was probably ripped. Self-doubt flooded over ever cell in me.

We decided to have dinner at this restaurant in the Village called *The Little Owl*. It was a trendy little restaurant that I had heard a lot about. I was surprised that David was able to get us in. Must have pulled strings with one of his Wall Street clients. The trapeze studio was in a warehouse-looking building over on the West Side Highway, so we met there.

"Kyle?" he said running his hands through his newly washed hair. He was beautiful. Not 6 feet tall, more like 5'5". Not dark haired, but light brown. Not blue eyes, but green. But nonetheless, he was beautiful. I could tell that his body was rock hard.

"David!" I said and we hugged. Yup. It was like hugging a statue. I felt flabby.

"Let's go to dinner!" We started across the highway, heading to the restaurant. It was a perfect early summer night. The air was warm, but it wasn't humid yet. Another couple of weeks and it would be dreadful. I never liked summer, much less in the city.

The Little Owl was charming. We had a table near the front. I couldn't stop looking at David. It was hard to believe he was sitting in front of me after months of emails and phone calls. I told him so. He agreed. It was great to finally meet.

I kept looking up at him over my menu. I could see him scanning the room and then his eyes stopped. There was a tall, dashing waiter standing near the bar. My heart sank a little. But thought, he's here with me. He asked me to dinner, not that guy. Just go with it. Just enjoy it.

"Thank you again for the magic you worked," he said, taking a sip of his water, his eyes again scanning the room. This time locked on a very distinguished looking man having dinner with what I assumed was his wife. Salt and pepper hair, perfectly dressed. Probably a dime a dozen for him in the Wall Street store. Maybe he developed a type from working there.

"I pulled a few strings. But, it was worth it," I said stupidly. He looked back and smiled at me. The rest of the meal, he was completely focused on me. Whew, I thought. There was hope for me.

When the check came, I insisted that I pay. I assumed that I made more money than he did since I was at corporate and he was at the store. Later, I thought about it and he probably made more than me on commission on all those suits and tuxedos. Whatever. I was happy to meet my crush and have a dinner with him in a charming restaurant.

Outside, we stood nervously, neither really sure of what the next step would be. We laughed and looked away from one another. Neither of us making a decision as we started walking. I wanted to take his hand in mine, but wasn't completely sure of myself.

"What do you want to do now?" I asked, looking like a kitten that begged to leave the shelter.

"I was thinking about going to *Splash*. We would both meet someone hot. What do you say?"

And there it is, I thought. The other shoe.

"No, I'm good. Thanks," I said. Of course, I didn't want to accompany my date to a gay bar so we could both meet someone else. I told him that I had a big report I had to prepare for Dick for the following day and that I needed to go. It was true, but I would generate the report in five minutes, as I was having my first cup of coffee. He shook my hand and tore off in the other direction.

I hailed a cab. I didn't feel much like walking. I got in and sunk down in the seat. I only looked at the rooftops of the buildings that we passed, my eyes dipping up and down, following the line from one building to the next. I couldn't stomach the thought of looking at all the beautiful people on the street. One of which, David would probably meet at

Splash and go home with. What's wrong with me? I thought.

David never called me again for help. At first, I was hurt, but then I realized it was for the best. I didn't want to hear from him either.

Trapeze? Really?

You're Not My Type #5

Friday. Oh, blessed Friday. It had been a particularly trying workweek dealing with Dick and now Friday was finally upon me. My Saturday plans, that I dreamt about all week, consisted of sleeping in, ordering brunch from my favorite spot, flipping through the New York Times, falling asleep on the sofa, placing a FreshDirect order, ordering dinner from the place I ordered brunch from and tackling the stack of Netflix next to the TV.

Friday night was another story. I had stayed late at work all week and was ready to go out. I didn't care about getting laid, I just wanted to go on a date. An old-fashioned, dinner and drinks, does he like me does he not the whole time, date.

I went online and I tried chatting up a guy named Paul. He was short, average looks, but seemed quirky and I thought we might have a nice time together.

Me: Hi! Great pic. Was wondering if you wanted to grab a drink after work?

After five minutes, Paul responded.

Paul: Not my type.

I shut down my computer, grabbed my coat and bag and left. While I waited for the elevator, I put on my khaki colored trench coat and slipped my cellphone into my bag. What was I going to do now? I didn't really feel like going home. I decided that I would find a bar and get myself a drink. I didn't need a date, right?

Bing. The elevator opened in the lobby and I exited with a sigh. I went through the turnstile and there he was. Paul. I recognized him immediately. He looked me head to toe, elevator style and made a grimace, shook his head and walked past me.

I pulled my bag up onto my shoulder and went through the revolving doors out into the crisp autumn air. Suddenly, I no longer felt like being around other people, so I found the nearest liquor store on my walk to the train. Vodka it was. Stoli. I normally drank red wine at home, but tonight, it was definitely vodka.

Fuck You

We had just installed a new digital tailoring system at *Books Brothers*. It was pretty cool, I have to say. You went into this little room, stripped down to your underwear and over 20,000 measurements were captured. These perfect, precise measurements were then emailed to a factory in Boston and six weeks later, a suit that you fit you like a glove, arrived. I was even so fortunate as to go through the process and Dick comp'd me a suit.

"Hey," he yelled as I was walking by his office. "C'mere."

"Yes?" I said, sitting down in the chair across from his desk.

"The New York Times is coming tomorrow to do an article on the new scanner."

"Ok,"

"So, I need you to wear the suit made from the scanner."

"That's not a problem."

"And don't talk to the press. I don't need you saying something stupid." Normally, I would have flinched at this, but this was Dick's new mode of communication. Suddenly, I found him aptly named.

Something had turned in him. In the beginning, I felt like I was on the fast track, just follow in his shadow and reap the rewards and benefits. And then, as if a switch were flipped, he became hypercritical of me.

"Is that seriously what you're wearing?" he cracked one day as I arrived at the office. At lunch, I went downstairs and bought a different dress shirt and tie.

Another time, we were in a meeting with all the various heads of departments and someone directed a question at me. I had a reputation of knowing all the floor managers and the sales associates so, I was often asked what the mood was like or if I had any insider information. Dick stopped me before I could respond. "Kyle doesn't know anything." I looked down at the big mahogany table, face turning bright crimson.

He must have seen my Kerry/Edwards button on the side of my bag and launched into a tirade about how all Democrats were pussies and wanted to take rich people's money and give it away to the lazy, poor. Just because he outfitted Manhattan's elite, he felt like he was one of them. He was a class act.

Vendors would have launch parties to showcase their new fabrics and he prohibited me from going. "I'll represent the department much better than you could." I got up and exited his office, no response. This pattern of abuse was the new normal. There wasn't anything I could do or say that he couldn't find fault with.

I often wondered if things were ok for him at home. He never mentioned his wife except to say that they had separate bedrooms in their new apartment and that they were trying to adopt a crackbaby. I thought, maybe you wouldn't have issues having a baby if you slept in the same bed. I secretly hoped his crackbaby would grow up to be addicted to meth and she'd steal all his money and cut the crotches out of all of his pants.

The day of the New York Times interview was the icing on this rotten cake. I greeted the reporter and photographer at the elevator. "Kyle?" said this pretty blond woman. I suspected she wasn't too much older than I was. I just nodded. Dick had specifically told me not to talk to these people. I wasn't going to chance it now. His closed-door office thrashings were now a daily occurrence.

"Dick Honeybell," he said extending his fat hand. God, I loathe you, I thought, smiling at the cameraman. "Right this way," he extended his arm in the direction of the digital scanner. They followed. The cameraman began setting up his equipment and Dick walked her through the process. She was bright and asked a lot of technical questions. I really wanted to correct Dick a couple of times when he told inaccuracies. But, I felt it was best to leave it be. No good would come from correcting him in public. I was actually trained by the company who designed and manufactured the scanning unit. I knew the thing inside and out. That didn't matter to Dick. There was a spotlight and he was damn well going to be in it.

"I would like to photograph someone going through the process, at every stage, to highlight the ease of using the scanner," said the reporter, turning to me. "Kyle. Would you mind us photographing you?"

Dick's face turned bright red and before a response could even enter my mind, he blurted out: "No! I'll call my friend Dan. He works in the building next door and he's attractive. More like the type of customer we'd like to attract." He turned, pulling out his phone to call Dan. I couldn't face looking at neither the reporter nor cameraman. I set my notebook down on the cash register next to the scanner and I left. I picked up my bag from my desk and I went home.

Two weeks later, I was fired. I was summoned into King Dick's office one last time. This time with a HR rep there. Very clinically, he handed me a sheet of paper and my eyes went immediately to the word TERMINATION. A huge sense of relief swept over my body, and was instantly followed with 'what am I going to do now?'

The HR lady walked me through the exit process and honestly, I didn't hear a word of it. I just kept glaring at Dick. After she was done, she asked if I had any questions. I shook my head, stood up and walked to the door. I couldn't help myself. I turned, looked Dick in the eyes and said: "Fuck you." Not my finest hour, but it felt great finally saying it.

You're Not My Type #6

Despite my track record with men, I decided to give it one more shot. I was lonely more than horny and chatted up a cute Italian guy named Jacob. I really just wanted to feel not alone. He was a few years younger than me, shorter than me and very skinny. He said I looked like fun, and probably against my better judgment, I invited him over.

I showered quickly and made my bed and fluffed and arranged the pillows on the sofa and chair. I sprayed my cologne on my V-neck tee and sat at the kitchen table waiting for him to arrive. Which he did, on-time. I like that, I thought.

I buzzed him in and he trekked up the four flights of stairs. I really hoped that Jack wasn't home and wouldn't open his door, seeing Jacob walking up to my apartment. Not that I had any explaining to do to him, it was just easier to keep my trysts to myself.

"Hey," he said, coming into my kitchen.

"Hey," I said back. He was hot. Very skinny. Too skinny. I thought I would break him in half. We shook hands and stood nervously for a few minutes. I offered him a drink. He declined. I offered him a seat in the living room. That he took me up on.

He flopped on the sofa and slouched down. I could see a giant bulge in his crotch. I was instantly turned on. I flopped down next to him. I started to gently caress his arm and he smiled. I leaned in for a kiss and he backed away. I sat back away from him as he fumbled in his pocket for something.

He pulled out a spoon, a baggie and a syringe. "Got a light?" he asked.

"Excuse me?" I said looking at his contraband.

"I thought you said you wanted to party."

"I thought you said you were going to take me *to* a party," I said in disbelief.

He quickly put away his equipment as fast as he had taken it out. "Look, I'm outta here. You're not my type anyway," he said bolting for the door.

I let out a sigh and thought to myself: Wow. I can't imagine having a drug habit that requires carrying around utensils.

Interrogation

Interviews are the worst. It's like dating, but you don't get fed or laid. I sat in the reception area and dried my palms on my suit pants. I checked the breast pocket of my jacket and found my compass. That made me smile.

People walking through the area looked on me with pity as they recognized I was there for an interview. The receptionist offered me water or coffee. I declined both. I flipped through *Really Easy* magazine and tried to anticipate questions that I would be asked. The magazine was launching a home product line and I was being interviewed for a position to develop those products.

What if this new boss was worse than Dick? I shuddered and rubbed my arms. That couldn't be possible. I hated the thought of being gun-shy and broken, but that's how I felt after Dick's abuse. Don't let it define you, I said, trying to prop myself up.

"Kyle?" a young assistant called out from behind an open frosted glass door.

"Yes," I said standing and buttoning my suit jacket. I was led through a series of hallways and again offered water or coffee. I accepted the water. I was shown into an all-white conference room and took my seat at the opposite side of the big table.

The assistant returned with the water and informed me that my interview would be a few minutes delayed because of a previous meeting. I swiveled a little in the chair and looked around the stark room. I could see various office workers running to and fro. I was trying to judge by their expressions and movements if I would fit in this space.

"Hi, Kyle," said an overweight, but very pretty lady. She waddled over and shook my hand as I stood.

"Hello," I said. "Thank you for taking the time to meet with me." We both sat. Her chair let out a wheezing sigh as the air escaped from the cushion.

"So, you are no longer at *Book Brothers*. What happened?" Boy, she wasted no time, I thought.

"My position was eliminated. My area was moved under the store operations department instead of product development." A lie, but it sounded plausible. She scanned me up and down as I spoke. I felt like I should have a spotlight on me and be surrounded by a group of 1940's detectives.

"I see," she said, looking at my résumé. "So, you have no experience working in home products."

I tried to fight back the knot in my throat. "No, but I have experience developing apparel products and am confident that experience would translate to home. And I have a passion for decorating and sewing." She scribbled something in the margin of my résumé.

"What experience do you have in merchandising product assortments?" She was tough.

"Well, part of my responsibility at *Books Brothers*, was to analyze the suiting and shirting offerings and rank them by performance and suggest replacements for those that were not working."

"So, what you're telling me is 'no'."

"Well, in a sense I have. Maybe not the scale, but the work was there."

"No," she said sternly, not taking her eyes off of mine.

"Ok," I said, not sure of what else I could say in that moment. We sat there in silence, eyes locked. This was weird.

"Do you have any experience working with product specs or designers?"

"Yes, as part of my internship, I would take the garment specs and check incoming shipments against them for any variances. I also worked closely with the designers to communicate this information and any comments I received from the stores."

"But, not for home products," she said more as a statement than question.

"No," I said softly, as if I had done something wrong. What had I done to make her dislike me after such a short period of time? I thought. I usually charmed people I just met. I wasn't handsome, but I could be charming at least. I was wasted on this woman.

"Why is it, do you think, that they didn't move you over into store operations when the department switched?"

I was caught completely off guard. I guess we're back to that. "I don't know. They had someone in store operations who worked in a similar function as me so that person got my work load." A lie, but I thought I saved myself.

"Uh huh," she said with clear disbelief. We sat again in silence. "Do you know anything about home product design?"

"Well, in college, when I was designing apparel collections, all of my mood boards and tear sheets were from interior design magazines. I should have put two and two together, that home product development was for me. That's where I am at now!"

"Why wouldn't you notice something so obvious about yourself?"

Ok. Now you're just being mean, I thought. "Well, everyone's lives travel at different paths and speeds. I got here so that's the main point."

Another cloak of silence fell upon us. She was tapping her red pen on the margin of my résumé, creating a pointillism design that made no sense.

"What assurances do I have that you won't leave us after accepting a position?"

"Well, there are no certainties in life. I would accept the position with an open mind and a positive attitude that it was going to work out."

She studied me for a moment longer, continuing to tap her pen against my résumé. "I think you are entirely wrong for this position, but I thank you for coming in." She dropped her pen, stood, waddled to the door and was gone. I sat in disbelief for a moment, looking at the corners of the room to see if I was on a hidden camera show.

"Kyle?" the assistant from earlier said. "I'll show you out." I grabbed my bag, zipped it up and followed her to the elevator banks. "Thank you!" she said, waving to me as the elevator doors shut.

What the hell had just happened? I asked myself as I watched the floor numbers descend to the lobby. I thought all my answers were spot-on. Maybe she had something go wrong in her personal life. Maybe her boss was mean to her. Oh, stop making excuses for her bad behavior. I scolded myself.

"Kyle?" a familiar voice beckoned behind me. I turned and my heart sank. There was Vinnie. J.Crew fitting room Vinnie.

"Vinnie!" I said, mustering as much cheer as I could.

"What are you doing?" he said hugging me. I didn't reciprocate the embrace.

"Oh, I just came from an interview. What about you?"

"I'm an assistant editor at *Really Easy*. In the food and wine department."

"That's great!" My heart sank further.

He held up his left hand. "My boyfriend and I just got engaged! Can you believe it?" My heart was now about to come out my ass.

"Congratulations!" I said, tears welling up in my eyes. "Listen, I've got to run, but it was great seeing you!"

"You too!" he exclaimed as I bolted. Out of view, I took out my cellphone and called *Really Easy* customer service.

"Hello," I said. "I'd like to cancel my subscription."

All Bets Are Off

It was one of those nights in New York that you look forward to all summer. The heat and humidity had passed, leaving a slight crispness in the air. My kind of weather.

I got out of a cab at Essex and Grand. Lower Manhattan has always confused me. To be perfectly frank, I'm lost below 14th street. I guess I'm a Midtown kind of guy.

The apartment was like that out of a movie or a window display. Perfectly karate-chopped pillows, picture frames full of friends and quirky moments lining the entry table, fresh cut flowers in every room. The host met me with an ear-to-ear grin. Lucas was strikingly beautiful. You knew at once that this perfect setting belonged to this perfect man.

"Come in," he welcomed. I handed him the bottle of wine I brought. Chet Baker played softly from somewhere in the living room. I could live here, I thought. I caught a glimpse of a photo of Greta Garbo on the wall next to the most exquisite armoire. I smiled.

"Where is everybody?" I asked nervously.

"Up on the roof. What are you drinking?"

"You have Campari?"

"Actually, I do." He motioned to follow him into the kitchen, a typical New York kitchen consisting of a sink big enough to wash your hands in and a stove half the size of a normal one. How does he making Thanksgiving dinner? I pondered. He took a glass from the cupboard and poured the drink. I stood there admiring his perfectly coifed jet-black hair, flawless olive skin, rock-hard pecs. He truly was beautiful. "Here you go." I accepted the glass and took a sip. "Let's go to the roof."

His apartment had direct access to the roof. A rare commodity. At the top of the stairs, I turned the corner and was met with all of lower Manhattan, up to the Empire State Building. The view was breathtaking. Joining the skyline was a bevy of people I have never met. A roof full of strangers. Nothing could have been more frightening. I sipped my drink and walked towards the first round of people I was introduced to.

I was at the party by the good graces of Barry, who insisted I meet Lucas, that we would be perfect for one another. Setups were hardly my specialty, but given my failures with on-line dating, I figured, why not. Barry and I didn't work out, so it was kind of him to suggest Lucas. Even though Lucas was way out of my league. Look, I'm well aware of my physical limitations in the gay community. I'm not appearing on billboards or high glossy print any time soon. I get it. And this seemed too good to be true.

"How are you, darlin'?" Barry asked, planting a kiss on both of my cheeks.

"I'm well. Good seeing you again." We made small talk and Barry brought me up to speed about an art opening he was going to after the roof party. I smiled at passersby and soaked in the scenery, the skyline and Lucas. This moment is definitely worth remembering, I thought.

After Barry departed, I thought I would take my leave as well. Lucas had another plan. "Stay. Please," he begged, his beautiful chocolate brown eyes melting me. There was no way I could refuse. I sat on a wooden bench and continued to enjoy my Campari and the twinkling lights of the buildings. I wondered who was occupying these skyscrapers on a Friday night and why they weren't they sitting on a roof deck, enjoying a beautiful stranger.

One by one, the roof cleared out until it was just Lucas and I. We sat for a bit in silence, both staring out in opposite directions, in thought. Every so often I would steal a glance at him. He seemed so cool and confident. He could have any guy in New York. Why me? This is the question that I wrestled with. Why not? Tumbled the other side of the argument. Why me?

"You are really beautiful," he blurted out. I choked a little on my drink and raised my eyebrows in disbelief. WHAT? "You are," he continued. "You are so different, there's something kind and gentle about you that adds to your hotness."

Ok. Hotness? Me? Clearly he was high on bath salts or something. I couldn't look at him. I was in uncharted territory and had no other plan, but to retreat into the recesses of denial. Ok, that sounded dramatic, but there was truth in there.

Before I knew it, he leaned in and kissed me. My entire body went flush with a tingling sensation. This isn't happening, I thought. He came back for a longer kiss and caressed the right side of my face.

"Follow me," he said as he stood up. I had a feeling I knew where this was going. Hand-in-hand, he led me back down to his apartment, past the armoire, past Greta, past the baby doll kitchen and into his bedroom.

There was a single candle burning on top of metal architect's drawers. It perfumed the room with an intoxicating honeysuckle smell and highlighted a wall full of black and white framed photographs of various building details. His bed looked like a cloud. Crisp white, with a very fluffy duvet, and piles of pillows. He turned and pulled me close, at the same time pulling my dress shirt out from my pants.

He kissed the side of my neck while holding my head in my hands. I couldn't help but explore his chiseled chest. It was magazine worthy. We began making out. He was the best kisser. "Is this happening?" I asked myself as we fell on the bed, him landing on top of me. The bed was as soft and inviting as it looked. He sat up on me and unbuttoned my dress shirt, kissing me after each button was loosened. I could hear Chet Baker playing "Tenderly" in the living room.

He pulled off his polo shirt to finally let me gaze upon that sculpted torso. I leaned forward and unbuttoned his jeans, releasing the largest penis I had ever encountered. I don't know where that is going, I thought. He collapsed on me again, planting kisses all over my neck while I ran my hands up and down his back. I inched my hand in between us to take him in my hands. It was huge. And limp. I started stroking him with the hopes of jumpstarting this process. But nothing happened.

With a sigh he rolled off me and pulled the covers over him. "I can't go through with this."

"With what?" I trembled.

"Look, you are really nice. You are. I can't sleep with you."

"Why not?"

He hesitated. I could tell there was a story behind that sigh. "Barry bet me that I couldn't go through having sex with you." My heart shot up through my throat and then down to my feet. What was I hearing? This had to be a bad joke and we would resume kissing any second. "And he's right. I can't. I am not into you."

I didn't know what to do, how to react so, I sat there. A few moments later, I could hear him snoring. It was faint, but he was definitely asleep. I looked at those beautiful pecs as I buttoned my shirt. Still in disbelief, I didn't move for what felt like an hour. Finally, I got up, blew out the candle, and left.

It's A Good Thing

What's next? I asked myself as I sat at my kitchen table, coffee in hand. I looked out the window at the building directly across and watched a man and wife (or girlfriend) frantically getting ready for work. After being dealt the blow of losing my job at *Books Brothers*, I tried to keep a normal routine. Watching this couple every morning made me feel like I was going to work too, that I had a sense of purpose beyond napping and *Grand Theft Auto*.

I opened my PowerBook and checked my email. Nada. Grrr. I took a sip of my coffee. The couple across the way had left. I liked having them there. Made me feel less alone. I hoped that they had a good day. I got up, sighed, stretched and walked over to the fridge to consider my breakfast options. The leftover Domino's was high on the list.

Ping! My inbox beckoned. There it was. The email I had so desperately been waiting for.

> From: Alana DeSantos [mailto:adesantos@marshastuart.com]
> Sent: 2/7/07
> To: Kyle Meyers
> Subject: Meeting
>
> Dear Kyle,
>
> I received your résumé and would like to invite you to meet with me. Please advise your availability this week.
>
> Best,
> Alana

After a couple quick email exchanges, my interview was set up for the following day. I sat back in the chair, amazed at how quickly my day had turned around. Nothing on the radar to suddenly an interview with a company that I adored and long admired. And now they wanted to meet me. *Me!*

Marsha Stuart (as we will call her here) is the country's best-known lifestyle guru. I remember flipping through copies of *Marsha Stuart Living* as a boy, in Wisconsin, dreaming of living like the pages full of antique china, perfectly pruned gardens, and exquisitely prepared food. It seemed like such a foreign world to me, considering we usually ate some form of flavorless meat on paper plates growing up. I was transported to a world of collecting milk glass, potting seedlings, making roman shades, setting the perfect table, crafting whimsical holiday cards, full of colors from the eggs her chickens would lay.

Looking around my apartment, Marsha's influence was everywhere. The paint, the mirror, the pillows, the candles and even my kitchen utensils bared her name. And now, I was being sought to help bring those very same products to market. Take that *Books Brothers*.

Immediately, I went into prep mode. Clothes were selected and pressed. Résumés were printed on the nicest paper I could find (and afford). Examples of my design work were arranged in a portfolio in case they were needed. I even took a photo of my impeccably tailored apartment, which, in my opinion, could have been shot for the magazine. Thank you cards were selected and addressed, ready to be filled out after the meeting. I was leaving nothing to chance.

Following the preparations, I called everyone in my address book to tell them about my interview. I hadn't been that happy in ages and it was nice to share good news for a change. My friends, knowing my obsession with Marsha, were over the moon for me.

Interview day came. I was early. I could see the Starett-Lehigh building across the avenues with its rows of huge windows and curved corners. It was the home to many designers, architects and photographers. It is situated on the West Side Highway, which is Manhattan's equivalent of middle of nowhere. Each avenue I passed, heading west, I thought, I would have to walk this every day? Then I quickly remembered that it was for Marsha Stuart!

I circled the block a couple of times to kill time. I was also scouting lunch spots or convenience store runs. Nothing. Just abandoned-looking warehouses. Lovely. Finally, it was time to go up. That and by this point, I was completely frozen.

After signing in and going through security, I was in the elevator, heading to the 9th floor. Just above the buttons was a sign that read: "HELP IS ON THE WAY." That made me smile, so I snapped a photo of it with my cellphone.

"Kyle Meyers for Alana," I announced to the young girl sitting behind a giant white glossy counter. Copies of the magazines lined the front of it. Everything was white. The walls, doors, window frames, even the floor was a bright glossy white. Simple soft gray benches and a plain white coffee table made up the reception area. A flat screen TV was mounted on the wall and played various clips from Marsha's daytime show. A single, simple vase of bright yellow daffodils was perched at the end of the counter.

"She'll be right with you. Please take a seat," said the receptionist.

I picked up the current issue of *Living* and began flipping through it. Closet makeovers, citrus marinades 101, classic casseroles reinvented, the merits of composting. "Kyle?" a voice inquired.

"Yes," I said, as I saw a beautiful young woman with flowing brown hair, Disney character eyes, Julia Roberts smile, in a perfectly tailored navy blue blazer and red jeans. Of course the HR representative would be beautiful.

"I'm Alana. Such a pleasure to meet you."

"Likewise!" I said, shaking her hand.

"Follow me," she said. We passed through reception, back out through the elevator area and she swiped her security card over a reader and opened the door. It was like peaking around Oz's curtain. I was finally behind the walls, the ultimate behind-the-scenes.

"Did you find the office ok?" she asked as we walked.

"Yes, no problems." We came upon her office, which was floor to ceiling glass and had a glass sliding door. All the offices were just like this one. Her desk was a simple white one. The chairs were made of the same grey leather as reception and were also very clean and stark. A single black and white image of cupped hands holding fresh-picked green beans hung on the wall behind her desk.

"Please, have a seat." And with that the interview began. It was like having a conversation with an old friend. Alana was so easy to talk to. Effortless really. She's really good at her job, I thought. I meticulously outlined how I was the best person to develop their new line of textiles that they were launching under a new upscale brand. Usually, first dates and interviews were beyond challenging for me. I was often tongue-tied and said "uh" in between every word. Not here. I was at the top of my game.

After the interview, she gave me a tour. Was this really happening?! I got to walk through the cavernous clerestory space in the middle of the office, full of light and echoes. I wandered through the prop library, photo studios, test kitchens, woodworking studio, past the rows of Internet programmers, prop stylists, editors (many of whom I recognized from the magazine). This alone was worth coming for, I thought.

"It was such a pleasure speaking with you," Alana said warmly as she held the door for me.

"You too!" She said she'd be in touch for next steps. This must have gone well! I got a tour after the interview and she's talking about next steps. I walked back to the subway, the entire way with a giant smile on my face, not caring about the slush, puddles and the chill in the air.

The following day, I received an email from Alana setting up the next interview with my would-be boss, Joseph, the Vice President of Merchandising. That meeting was scheduled for the following week.

The day of the interview, a snowstorm hit the city. I checked my phone and my email and no sign of the interview being canceled, so I bundled up and headed over to the meeting. Each block closer to the river, the snow piled higher and higher. Apparently, shoveling the sidewalks in front of the art galleries and warehouses wasn't a priority for the city. By the time I got to the building, my pants below the knee were soaked and my feet sloshed around inside my dress shoes. It was really a miracle I didn't fall and break something.

"Hi, Kyle!" said Alana, greeting me at reception. "So sorry to make you come out in this weather!"

"No problem!" I exclaimed, teeth chattering. How did she not look like a drowned rat like me? She must have taken a cab. I should have.

"Can I get you water or coffee?"

"Coffee would be wonderful." Normally, I rarely accept beverages at interviews for fear of dumping them all over myself, but I needed the coffee to warm up.

We made a pit stop at a tiny, glossy white kitchen where she poured me a cup of coffee into a shiny white mug. So much white.

"Milk? Sugar?" she asked.

"Black." She handed me the cup and lead me to Joseph. He was shorter than me, slicked back jet-black hair, wire frame glasses and a welcoming smile.

"Such a pleasure meeting you!" he said, extending an offer to sit at the chair opposite his.

"I'll leave you two to talk," said Alana, sliding the glass door shut. Joseph had an inspiration wall opposite his desk with hundreds of various home products pinned to the board. I wondered what Marsha thought of that. Would she perceive it as clutter?

We began talking about my background and my love of the brand. Like with Alana, it was easy and familiar speaking with him. I looked at the white mug on the desk and thought of an article in the recent issue that featured Marsha's new kitchen remodel at her house in Bedford. I loved how she had stacked the Drabware cups and saucers in her cabinet. I told Joseph that inspired me to do the same with mine.

"That's excellent!" he said. He wrapped up the interview by thanking me for coming out in the middle of a snowstorm and showed me to the elevators. I trudged back to my apartment in the storm, replaying our meeting in my mind. I should have offered to set my mug back in that kitchen, I thought. Oh, well. I went home and changed out of my waterlogged suit and wrote him a thank you card.

A few weeks had passed and I thought of writing Alana to check in. Maybe things hadn't gone as smoothly as I thought! Before I could, my phone rang.

"Kyle?" asked Alana.

"Hi, Alana, how are you?"

"Very well, thank you. Listen, I'm calling with good news! We would like to offer you the position of Product Manager."

And with that, I was now part of an elite group of talented, creative and ambitious people. I was in. I had landed my dream job. I couldn't believe it. I felt like I was living in a dream with the edges of every surface glowing. I emailed

my entire address book the good news and celebrated with
lunch at Taco Bell.

You're Not My Type #7

"Sorry. Not my type." The words came across my phone.
I was to meet Max at Madison Square Park for a late lunch
at Shake Shack. I stood there, long past our scheduled time
until finally I gave up and started to walk back to my place.
I don't know which is worse, I thought, being stood up or
being told you aren't someone's type. Or both. I stopped
in Lenny's Bagels and got a chicken salad sandwich and a
Diet Coke for the walk home. As I nibbled my sandwich, I
looked at the men that I passed and thought am I your type?
What about you?

Back at my apartment, I dropped my bag to the floor,
kicked off my shoes and went to my computer. I was
hoping to find an explanation why we had chatted for
weeks, exchanged photos and suddenly, Max was no longer
into me. And he clearly was there, in the crowd, getting a
good look at me. Let it go, I thought.

In a chat room, I said hi to this beautiful Middle Eastern
looking guy named Zach. "Not my type," he wrote back. I
responded with: "You could at least say 'Hello, not my
type'?" Where were people's manners? Geesh! "Fuck
you," he wrote back and promptly blocked me.

I tried my luck with this adorable, overweight Jewish guy
named Adam. "Not my type," he too, responded. I closed
the chat window. I couldn't hear that sentence one more
time. Seriously? Was I anyone's type?

What's In A Name?

Stories about Marsha were legendary. We all had
them. And we would love to regale one another with any
new additions to the canon of tales. I met Marsha, for the
first time, at a party thrown for the departing Vice President
of Design. I got tipsy on white wine and begged someone
to introduce us. She seemed indifferent and shook my hand
with her man-sized hand.

Over the next three years of my employment, I would have
several run-ins with her. The first was when I was
inspecting a pillow sample that had arrived from our retail
partner. She was walking by and saw me looking at it, took
it from my hands and told me that she didn't like the
stitching, that it needed to be cleaned up. I assured her it
would be. It was a done deal, however. The goods were
already on a boat headed for America.

During a meeting with the teams, I was barked at to fetch a
sample from the sample closet. As I went to get it, I ran
into Marsha, giving an office tour to a couple of people, as
she often did. There was no easy way for me to get around
them so I retreated and walked behind. "The space opened
in 2000 and as you can see now, it's a complete
shithole." I bit my lip and our eyes met. "Wouldn't you
agree, Kyle?" she looked to me for confirmation. "It could
be a bit tidier in here," I concurred.

Another time, she stopped at my desk on the way to her
office and said: "I want 18 sets of green sheets sent to my
house in Maine." And walked away. I scrambled for the
phone to get any details out of her assistant. Sizes? Which
green? When? How were they being paid for? "I don't

know, just make it happen!" her assistant squealed and hung up the phone.

Her explosions were unforgettable. We had a design review once where our design director presented a red, polyester damask comforter to her. It had been a request from the retailer that we fought them tooth and nail on and finally gave in, after they revealed how much retail revenue it represented. Marsha was just seeing it for the first time.

"It looks like casket lining." I tried not to laugh. Someone in the group did, which enraged her. "Would you put your fucking name on this?" No, the person muttered. She then went around the room and asked each of us the same question, all with the same answer. "Then why is my fucking name on it!?" she screamed at the top of her lungs, echoing throughout the clerestory as she stormed off.

Another time she referred to the spout of a teakettle as looking like an infant's penis. Upon inspecting stainless steel mixing bowls that she felt weren't up to her standards, she dropped them each to the ground and stomped them inside out. Displeased with the quality of whisks we designed, she took every sample we had, bent them all out of shape and threw them across the office. I picked one up and kept it in my desk drawer and would laugh every time I saw it. A kind of crazy touchstone.

But, my favorite Marsha moment was a funny one. Twice a year we would set up the clerestory space to look like a mock retail environment, complete with fixtures and signage to highlight the product offerings for that season. It was a big deal. The press walked through it and buyers placed their orders based on the presentation. Directly off the clerestory, was this large space we would use for meetings and as a staging area to open the boxes and arrange product before setting it on the fixtures out in the clerestory.

I was working late. Before calling it a night and heading home, I needed to go to the bathroom. In doing so, I had to walk through the staging area to get to the restroom. I turned the corner to find Marsha standing there, by herself, loading up her Birkin bag with samples. Appetizer plates, wooden spoons, trivets, acrylic glassware. My first thought was, those aren't food safe! My second thought was, you are so cheap!

Our eyes met and she shrugged me off: "What? My name's on it."

A Focus On Wiping

"You should totally meet my friend, Roger! You two would totally hit it off," said Nina, my coworker at Marsha Stuart.

"Really?" I said, not taking my eyes off my spreadsheet. I knew what this was. This was a classic case of "I have a gay friend and you are gay so therefore you would be perfect for one another."

"Yes! He's our age, he's cute, he's funny. You'd like him." This prospect was getting better. A little.

"Oh?" I said, turning to see Nina holding out her cellphone with an image of a guy on it. I took it from her. He was cute. She was right. "What if he doesn't want to meet?"

"He will! He hasn't had a boyfriend in year." Red flag.

"Ok," I surrendered.

An email blast came through, the body of the email contained in the subject line:

> From: Corporate Communications [mailto:corpcomm@marshastuart.com]
> To: all_corporate
> Date: 5/14/07
> Subject: MARSHA TEN MINUTES OUT. CLEAN OFFICE NOW.

With that, began a series of frantic drawers being opened and stuff dumped in them, people clearing surfaces of everything, housekeepers running every direction. Marsha lived up to her perfectionist image. Legend had it that one day, as she was entering the office, she noticed flowers on an assistant editor's desk that were starting to wilt. She stopped dead in her tracks, pointed at them and screamed: "DEAD FLOWERS!" She then proceeded to dump the entire thing, vase and flowers, into the trash and fired the editor. I never really feared these walkthroughs because I kept my desk to a minimalist perfection.

"Are you free this Thursday?" asked Nina. Of course I was. My life consisted of going to work, coming home, cycling through my regular rotation of take-out places and watching Netflix.

"Yes." And a few moments later, I had confirmation that Roger and I were meeting.

I found an empty bench in Union Square Park and sat down. I took out my phone and started a game of solitaire to avoid talking to the approaching homeless man. Of course, I was early.

"Kyle?" said Roger.

"Roger!" I said standing up. He looked exactly like his photo. That never happens. "How are you?"

"I'm well. You?"

"I'm well," I said shaking his hand. "How do you know Nina?" I asked out of nervousness.

"Oh, I was friends with her roommate in college."

"Gotcha. So, should we head to dinner?"

"Actually, do you mind a little adventure before dinner?" Another red flag.

"What kind of adventure?"

"Trust me. It'll be fine." He turned and started to walk across the park and I followed suit. We walked in silence over the avenues to 15th and 7th. What was this adventure? We were in Midtown so what could this possibly be? He took out a sticky note and double-checked the address that we had stopped in front of. "This is it," he announced.

Was it a sex party? Was it a poetry reading? Worse. "We're here for the focus group," Roger said to the bubbly, blond curly haired girl behind the desk.

"Great!" she said and mechanically handed us both a clipboard and pen. "Please take a seat and fill out these waivers and confidentiality agreements."

This was seriously happening? We sat on a rustic looking wooden bench and filled out our forms. When finished, Roger took mine and handed them back to the receptionist. "Great!" she bubbled.

We sat in awkward silence as four more guys arrived and filled out their paperwork. Dear God, what was the subject of this focus group? I almost bolted for the door, but though of facing Nina at work the next day after Roger filled her in. They are just going to ask you a few questions and then you can go, I told myself.

A tall man, probably in his early fifties with salt and pepper hair and dressed like Mr. Rogers, came into the reception area. "Gentleman! Please follow me." He led us through the office, which appeared to be an advertising agency. Everything looked like it was made from reclaimed wood with black metal accents. Kind of chic, I thought. He led us into a room with a camera on a tripod and three sofas forming a U-shape. My last moments on Earth are going to be in this room, recorded on that camera, I thought.

"Please, take your seats."

Roger smiled as we sat down next to one another. Once we were seated, the tall man continued. "Great. Thank you for participating in this focus group. We have a client that is about to launch a very exciting new product and we would like to get your feedback on your daily habits." Ok. This wasn't so bad. "That is," he continued. "Your habits with wiping." And on cue, he held up a roll of toilet paper. Where did that come from? I thought.

I looked over at Roger and gave him a look that was somewhere between "Hi!" and "Seriously?" He smiled eagerly back at me.

"How many times a day do you have a bowel movement?" asked the tall man. One by one we went around the room. "Two," I said.

"Great! I have to ask the age old question, do you put your toilet paper on the roll facing over or under?" "Over," I said.

"Great! Do you use toilet paper to wipe or do you use moist towelettes or other personal hygiene products?" "Toilet paper," I said. So far, Roger and I had the same bathroom habits. Maybe this could work.

"Ok. When you wipe, how many squares of toilet paper do you use at a time?" "Six," I said. Roger concurred. I wondered if he was telling the truth or he was giving answers to align with me on our first date.

"When you are wiping, do you go up into the anus or strictly stay outside it." Ok. Where was this headed? "In," I said. I mean, cleanliness is next to godliness right? Roger stayed on the surface. I don't know why but this skeeved me out.

The tall man continued to ask us questions about wiping and our bowel movements. Did we prefer 2 ply versus 1 ply? Did we like scented or unscented? Bleached versus all natural paper? How long did our average bowel movement take? I learned that Roger preferred quilted 2 ply, unscented, bleached and he was on the pot for no more than three minutes at a time. I thought, well, that's good at least if I had to go and he was using the bathroom. I wouldn't have to wait very long.

We were thanked for our participation and each handed a plain white envelope. Inside was a fifty dollar bill. Suddenly, I felt very cheap, getting paid to talk about my poo.

"So, dinner. How does *Hill Country* sound?" Roger said, holding the door for me as we left the building.

"Sure," I said, buttoning my coat as I hit the chill in the night air.

Hill Country was pretty close by. Soon we were feasting on various cuts of smoked and barbecued meat, potato salad and drinking Long Island Iced Tea out of Mason jars. We didn't really talk during dinner. What was left to say? He kept licking his fingers as he ate his ribs. I could only picture him sitting on the toilet. For no more than three minutes.

After dinner, we parted with a simple handshake. As soon as he was out of sight, I immediately coated my hands with sanitizer. I never saw Roger again. But, I still have my Jonathan Adler designed toilet paper cover.

Romance, Arkansas

Our retail partner approached us to create a line of candles, room sprays and potpourri that would be sold under Marsha's name. I have long adored candles, always having one burning in my apartment. Candlelight is so relaxing and everyone looks better by it.

My counterpart on the retail side was this larger than life woman named Mary. She was this outspoken Jewish woman in her late 40's with the biggest hair I have ever seen. And it never moved. Ever. She always had a knack for saying the most inappropriate comments. She was dynamic. Upon meeting her, you had no idea what to do with her, but you knew you liked her.

"Do you mind going on this trip?" Joseph asked me during our weekly touch base meeting.

"Of course!" I exclaimed. My first business trip! This was so exciting. "Where am I going?"

"Arkansas." He must have seen my face drop. "It will be fun! You're traveling with Mary." I perked back up.

We agreed to meet at LaGuardia airport. Mary and I were accompanied by Jasmine, a beautiful designer from Turkey who worked with me at Marsha and Katie, Mary's soft-spoken Italian assistant. This was our group.

"Ma'am," said a really menacing looking TSA agent to Mary. "Ma'am, you can't take this on the plane." He was holding up the biggest can of Aquanet I've ever seen.

"No, no, no, no, no. You've got to be kidding me! Do you think this hair looks like this on its own?" she yelled, tugging at that immovable coif.

"Mary," I intervened. "We can stop in Arkansas and get you a new can." She relented knowing that her confiscated can wasn't the last one on the planet.

"Here we go!" she said with a thick, twangy accent. An obvious nod to our destination. Jasmine smiled nervously. She was so uptight and serious that I couldn't wait to see she and Mary together. This is going to be good, I thought. Katie just rolled her eyes, used to her boss's antics.

Arriving in Arkansas, Mary got the rental car and we started our hour-long drive to the company, Aromatix, who produced a bunch of different home fragrance lines. It was located in Romance, Arkansas. Dotted along the way, were several points of interest that had us cracking up in the car: *Xtreme Taxidermy* (what makes it extreme, we wondered), a store named simply *Pageant Gowns*, and a chain of convenience stores under the name *Smitty's* that boasted on their signs that they sold ammo and cupcakes. They had a replacement can of Aquanet for Mary.

"Romance, Arkansas," said Mary in that same thick twang. "I could use me some of that there romance!" I busted out laughing. Jasmine even cracked a smile. "And a pageant gown."

When we pulled into Aromatix, we were greeted by two very tall women, both with Dorothy Hamill haircuts, white turtlenecks, black jumpers, bright pink lipstick and necklaces that looked like voodoo charms. "They are going

to keep our bodies in a freezer in the basement." I
whispered.

"How y'all doin'?" said Pauline, the owner. "This here's
Janice. And I'm Pauline." We shook their hands and were
shown into their offices. The receptionist was wearing the
same white turtleneck and black jumper. "We must not
have gotten the memo," I whispered to Mary.

We sat down in a conference room with no windows.
Wood paneling lined the walls along with paintings of
pheasants and foxes and an actual deer, antelope, and a
taxidermy bear. I leaned in and saw the *Xtreme Taxidermy*
logo on the deer. They love their taxidermy.

For the next two hours, we picked botanicals for the
potpourri, selected the candle vessels and smelled over
three hundred vials to select the fragrances. Needless to
say, we were loopy. I thought of Betty and the Sharpies in
the supply closet. "Well, let's git you to yer hotel and we'll
have dinner," Pauline said, closing her notebook.

"Where are we staying?" asked Jasmine. I pictured a rusty
mobile home in the woods.

"It's a beautiful hotel called Green Apple Inn. And I own
it." Of course you do, I thought. We needed to take two
cars now that our group had increased by two. "Kyle!
Why don'tchu ride with me!" Pauline squealed.

"Ok," I muttered, locking eyes with Mary and mouthing the
words "Help me." Pauline drove an S-class Mercedes-
Benz. It was the nicest car I had ever been in. I closed the
door with a solid thud and buckled my seatbelt. I looked
back at the other car and longed to be with them. Why

couldn't Janice ride with Pauline? Off we went and after a few minutes of uncomfortable silence, Pauline broke it.

"I've got lots of gay friends you know," she said.

Wow, I thought. "Oh?" I said.

"Yep! And they sure can cut my hair!" Oh, stereotypes, I thought.

We pulled onto a long, winding road that went through the middle of a golf course. I could see a sprawling wooden structure in the distance.

"This is my golf course, The Green Apple Links."

"Very nice," I said. She must own the county, I thought.

We stopped at the entrance to the hotel and I jumped out before the hotel porter could open my door. I ran to the rental car and opened Mary's door. "She told me she's got lots of gay friends." I whispered.

"Oh, God," said Mary, shaking her head.

Our rooms were very beautiful. Each with a working fireplace and a giant bowl of granny smith apples. My room faced this sprawling valley, completely green and lush. The only sound I could hear was a bird calling from afar and twigs breaking under some animal walking in the woods. I let out a sigh and took a big breath of that air. My gaze drifted to the big valley and thought, this is *Deliverance* country. I washed my face and went to the lobby to meet the others for dinner.

The restaurant was decorated in the same style as their offices – lots of animal oil paintings and stuffed ones, too. "The steak here is rul good," said Pauline.

"Yes! Git whatever y'all want," chimed Janice. Mary kicked me under the table and I had to bite my lip not to smile. We ordered the steak, Katie the chicken and Jasmine the fish. Mary and I each also ordered a much-needed martini.

"We don't have any *I-talians* here in Romance." Pauline said looking at Katie. "But, I do love me a mean lasagna!"

Wow, I thought. Mary kicked me again under the table.

"I don't know how you live up there in New York City with all them Jews and Blacks." No one spoke. We all sat there, wide-eyed, staring at the person across from one another. Aside from an African American and an Asian person, everyone was represented at that table. Both Mary and Jasmine were Jewish, Katie was Italian and I am gay. Thank God, Pauline likes her Dorothy Hamill cut. Speaking of which, what self-respecting gay man would cut her hair like that? I shuddered.

No one spoke a word after that. Our food came and again we were stunned, locking eyes with one another. Each of our plates looked absolutely identical - a breaded, fried strip of protein, green beans just turning an olive color and a huge dollop of mashed potatoes.

"I ordered the fish," spoke Jasmine in her demure, delicate accent.

"That is the fish!" exclaimed Janice. Jasmine took her fork and scraped off the breading to reveal the fish. Nancy and I did the same to ours to discover steak. "We love our breadin'!" said Janice, proudly. I took a huge gulp of my martini and watched my fellow diners scrape all the breading off their food. The mashed potatoes weren't bad, but my chicken-fried steak was cooked just short of being leather.

After dinner, we excused ourselves and sprinted to our rooms. Maybe I was being dramatic, but I wedged a chair under my doorknob and locked it. I pictured the village showing up with torches. I didn't really sleep that night, maybe it was the quiet I wasn't used to or maybe it was the fear of being tarred and feathered.

The next morning, we piled into the rental and Jasmine said: "Step on it! Get out of here!" Mary wasn't going to argue with that and we tore out of there. So much so, that we got pulled over by a state trooper for speeding.

"What's yer hurry?" the officer asked.

"We've got a flight to catch," offered Mary, looking for some sympathy.

"Uh huh," he said taking out his ticket pad. "I'm still gonna hafta give ya'ticket."

"Ok, fine, but write fast." I kicked the back of Mary's seat. She grabbed the ticket, threw the car into drive and took off. We were able to get on an earlier flight that we all welcomed. I was about to fall asleep when the flight attendant announced they were coming around with snacks for purchase. On point, Mary stood up, waved a half-eaten bag of Twizzlers and said: "Candy, $2! I'll beat her price!"

You're Not My Type #8

Central Park was in full bloom. Everything was green and bright and colorful flowers lined the winding paths. I could make out sneezes here and there as I walked. Allergy season was upon us. I had wandered far enough into the park that I couldn't see any buildings above the trees. It made me feel like I was back in Wisconsin, wandering through my grandmother's forest next to our dairy farm.

I found a vacant bench, our designated meeting spot and sat down. I took the earbuds to my iPod out and put them in my pocket. I was to meet Andy there. I really wanted him to just come to my apartment, but he insisted on meeting first before we hooked up. Promptly at 3 p.m., I saw him walking towards the bench. I recognized him from his photo, even though the photo was easily four years old.

"Hey," he said as I stood up from the bench.

"Hi," I said. We stood there, awkwardly, for a few minutes. He wasn't making eye contact with me. Maybe he was just shy. Maybe he didn't do this often. "Should we start walking?" I asked. He nodded and we started wandering, not speaking.

We wandered and meandered. Not speaking. He must be really shy, I thought. I could tell that we were nearing the edge of the park as 5th Avenue was coming into view. This was good. We were probably headed to his apartment to get this started. We stopped under a tree, across from a very expensive looking apartment building. The doorman pacing in front in his burgundy and gold suit.

"Look," he said and my heart sank. "I can't do this. I'm just not into you." I nodded and turned before another word could be said. I headed down 5th Avenue, pretending to look in the shop windows that I passed, so the tourists wouldn't see my tears.

Dingleberries

Meetings with our retail partner were always tense. They thought they understood the Marsha Stuart brand better than we did and they often developed products without our knowledge and surprised us by putting them up for sale, leaving us no recourse. We were also pitching products with a very sophisticated taste level. Not something they did well. It was a constant battle and often ended with someone screaming.

The retail partners all sat in order of rank. They were very hierarchal. We just sat wherever there was an open seat. And we didn't just have meetings. We had a pre-meeting to discuss the meeting. And then after the meeting, we'd have a follow-up meeting. Sometimes, if it was a particularly tense subject, we would have pre-pre-meetings and post-post-meetings. It was the bane of my existence.

My job was to find a location, which was never easy. One time, I held a meeting in reception because no conference rooms were available. Another desperate time, I asked if I could use one of the photo studios. "You can, but we'll have to charge your department the day rate for the space," the studio manager said. "It's for a company meeting!" I said shocked.

I arranged chairs, put printouts and recaps on the chairs, made sure anything we didn't want the retailers to see was put away. This particular day, I was in luck, that the design area was free. I got in early and cleared the surface, set out the white folding chairs and put the design boards in order of product category. We were starting with bedding, then bath, and then utility bedding, which consisted of pillows, comforters and blankets. We had four hours blocked out on the calendar, but we knew it was going to be an all-day affair. I preemptively asked Joseph's assistant to order lunch for the group.

My phone rang. It was reception. The group was ready. It consisted of Buyers, Senior Buyers, Assistant Buyers, Product Managers, Senior Product Managers, Assistant Product Managers, Designers, Assistant Designers, and the Vice Presidents of the respective areas. Total head count was 18 people. On our team was myself, Joseph and our Vice President of Design, Natalie.

Natalie was a tall, beautiful British woman with wavy chocolate brown hair, crystal blue eyes, full, sensual lips and flawless fair skin. She was always impeccably dressed and had the most delightful accent. She had a natural charm and grace about her. She was the perfect person to present our concepts to the retailer.

"Natalie, they're here," I said, sticking my head into her office.

"Bloody hell," she said, standing up from her desk and flattening out her Prada dress. "I can't deal with these people today."

"Tell me about it," I said as we walked together to the design area where everyone was waiting.

The meeting went very well, comparably so to other meetings. Around 2 p.m., we started discussing utility bedding as we ate lunch. This wasn't the sexiest of categories and we were always challenged from a design perspective to provide newness. After color updates to blankets and the addition of a body pillow, we came to throws. We had a great selling throw that was a solid color with both ends dotted with pompoms.

"And now we are up to this guy," Natalie said, pulling the design board forward, showing all the additional colors we were suggesting doing the throw in. "Since the dingleberry blanket has done so well for us, we are only suggesting color updates." There were a few snickers from the crowd. I couldn't believe my ears. Around the office, we all affectionately referred to them as dingleberries. Natalie heard us a hundred times call it that.

"I just love dingleberries and they have performed very well for us and are very much on brand." Mary busted out laughing, causing Natalie to slow down her presentation. "We…we could also try multicolored dingleberries. That might be fun." It just kept going. My face was bright red. By now, pretty much everyone in attendance was snickering.

"Go tell her what it means," whispered Joseph to me. I made my way to the front and cupped my mouth to Natalie's ear. Immediately, every cell in her body was the same bright red as her lipstick.

"Oh, my God! I can't believe I was talking about bits of poo!" she shrieked.

Everything sounds better with an English accent.

Over Too Soon

Marsha Stuart had a new cookbook out and I had to have it. It was a compilation of easy, weeknight meals. I had every book she published and I was compelled to keep my collection complete. From hors d'oeuvres to home keeping to crafting, I had them all. Thirty-two books.

Barnes and Noble at Union Square was crowded. More so than usual. I made my way upstairs to the cookbook section. There it was, stacked front and center on the first table off the escalator. I picked up the copy on top and began flipping through it. The images and layout of the recipes were perfect. Chicken Parm, Spicy Thai Noodle Soup, Steak with Peppercorn Sauce. My stomach started to growl. I was sold.

Closing the cover, I turned to head to the checkout line. I noticed a tall, lanky, blond, curly haired guy standing next to me. Was he even old enough to drink, I asked myself. He was wearing a tight, red polo shirt, dark jeans and flip-flops. He had a copy of Marsha's book in his hand, too.

"Isn't the book great?" he asked me.

"I'm so excited to cook from it," I said, quickly looking away. I was never good with strangers.

"I love to cook. I'm not very good at, I confess. But, that doesn't stop me." I chuckled at his honesty.

"Marsha is the reason I can cook at all," I admitted. He smiled. He was adorable.

"I'm Sam," he said, extending his hand.

"Kyle," I returned, shaking his hand.

"What do you do when you're not cooking?" he asked me confidently.

"I actually work for Marsha Stuart. I develop her home textiles. Bedding and bath stuff."

"You're shitting me?!"

"Honest!" I said, taking my employee card from my wallet as proof.

"What's she like?" he asked. This was the question that immediately followed any time I told someone that I worked for her.

"Let's just say, her reputation proceeds her." He laughed. "What do you do?"

"I'm a student at The New School. Film Production." I thought of Nicholas. My heart sank a little.

"Well, I should pay for this," I said, flashing Marsha his way, and started walking to the checkout line.

"Um, what's the first recipe you're going to make?" he said from behind me.

I turned, "I don't know. Probably the Chicken and Biscuits. I'm a sucker for comfort food."

"Me too." He smiled. I could see him drying his palms on the sides of his jeans, switching the book from right to left hand. Why was he nervous? It was me!

"What about you?" I asked.

"Definitely the Lemon Garlic Chicken."

"Excellent choice." I smiled and turned back to face the counter. It was my turn to pay.

Outside, I stopped to put the bag around my wrist and was about to cross the street to head to Whole Foods when Sam tapped me on the shoulder.

"I, um, was wondering if you wanted to get a drink?" he asked as I noticed beads of sweat forming on his upper lip. Bless his heart, I thought.

"Can I ask a question? I mean, I don't want to sound rude, but are you old enough to drink?"

He laughed. "Yes, I'm 22." God. A baby, I thought. Why not?

"Sure, where do you want to go?"

"I know a little dive bar near my school. We could go there." He had me at dive bar.

We crossed the street, our matching shopping bags on either side of us. We didn't really speak and that was ok. We both looked around at all the food vendors and the various products they were selling. I asked if it was ok if we stopped so I could buy a loaf of bread and Sam agreed. He selected the same bread as me. "My treat," I said as I took it from his hands and set it on the table.

"This is it," he said as we stopped in front of a nondescript bar called "Johnny's." It looked like it remained completely unchanged since 1960. I held the door for him. The inside matched the outside. Opposite the bar were red vinyl booths held together in places with grey duct tape. Above them were framed photographs of the bar throughout the years and the regulars who have come and gone. We each plopped down on matching red vinyl stools. Mine had a sharp edge that cut into my leg.

"You ok?" Sam asked.

"Oh, I'm fine," I said, rubbing my leg. A heavyset, older guy finished wiping his hands with a bar mop, came over to us.

"What can I getcha?" he asked.

"I'll have a Campari and soda." I could see the bright red bottle behind the bar so I knew I was safe to order it.

"I'll have a Cosmo," said Sam. Clearly a new drinker, I thought.

"I'm going to see your ID," said the bartender. We both reached for our wallets. "Not you," he said to me. Did I look that old? I sighed.

"So, where are you from?" I asked.

"Rhode Island."

"Oh! I love Rhode Island. Such a beautiful state."

"Yeah, I like it here. I'm far enough away from my family, but close enough that if I need to go home, it's only a few hours away."

"I'm from Wisconsin." He smiled and put his hand on my knee. We sipped our drinks and talked for about an hour. He pressed me for details about working for Marsha. I pulled out my usual stories, which he ate up like a kid on Christmas morning. He kept his hand on my knee, taking it off only when other patrons would pass by. I thought he was really sweet.

"I, um, don't normally do this, but, um, do you want to go back to my room?" he trembled.

"Sure," I said, finishing the last of my drink.

His dorm was close by. I got signed in and we got in the elevator. I immediately thought of my dormitory days. This was much nicer.

"I've got my own room. So, we'll be ok," he said. I smiled. He took my hand with his and rubbed the top of it with his thumb. His eagerness was so adorable. "Here it is," he said, unlocking the door. There was a sign with his name on, it in construction paper, clearly made by his R.A.

His room was pretty standard. A honey colored veneered desk and matching chair, twin bed pushed against the wall, a Coldplay poster pinned above it, a pile of clothes next to a dresser. The top of it was lined with bottles of cologne.

He closed the blinds and turned on the box fan next to the dresser. I guess he was warm. He nervously came up to me and kissed me. He was a really good kisser. We stood there, kissing for what seemed like forever. He pulled my

T-shirt off as I dropped my jeans to the floor. He did the same. I noticed a scrape on my leg from the barstool. We continued our make-out session. I could feel him against me and noticed a huge wet spot on his briefs.

The moment of truth came. We both slid off our underwear. He had a beautiful penis. It could have been on a statue in any museum. I kind of pinched myself. Here I was in this kid's dorm room. It all felt so wildly naughty.

"Come here," I said, kissing him and taking that beautiful penis in my hand. I was met with a groan and a palm full of gunk. I looked down at my hand, dripping in cum.

"Um, um, I am so sorry." His face was instantly red. I stepped back and he grabbed a towel off the pile of laundry on the floor and handed it to me. "I have a problem. Sorry," he said, not looking at me. My heart broke for him.

"That's ok. Don't worry about it! I should be flattered." I tried to encourage him.

"Here, I will take care of you." I was no longer hard.

"I'm good. Don't worry about me," I said, pulling my underwear back up.

"Sorry," he said, again not looking at me. I kissed his cheek and assured him it was ok. We got dressed in an awkward silence. He walked me down to the front desk and signed me out. Cookbook and bread in hand, I began my walk back to my apartment. I realized that Sam and I hadn't exchanged numbers. Oh, well, I thought. He's too young. Yeah, that was it.

You're Fired

Joseph was out. Just like that. My boss and mentor of two years was gone. Nina and I were devastated. We sat at our desks and stared at each other, deer-in-the-headlight style, neither of us speaking. I could see Joseph packing up his desk and seven years of memories. My heart broke for him.

"Nina! Kyle! In here! Now!" barked Patty, my boss's boss and I guess now, by default, our new boss. "Close the door," she said, sitting down and throwing her reading glasses off as she did. "I wanted to take a moment to tell you that now that Joseph is gone, you both will be reporting directly into me. There are no plans to fill his position." Neither of us said a word. I don't even think we were blinking. "Any questions?" Silence. "Good," she said with a tone that meant 'now get the fuck out of my office.'

Joseph waved a small wave at us as he shut off the lights to his office. He looked like he had just been hit by a truck. Why was Patty getting rid of him? We loved him!

Patty had a long and sordid reputation in the industry. She brought results, but it came at a price and never without casualties. Her main mode of communication was yelling. I was in a taxi once with her when she made the cabby cry. She was an expert at putting people on edge, beating them down and then getting whatever it was that she was out for. Usually, it was the jugular. Rumors circulated that she was a lesbian, but I thought that was just a stereotype. I saw her as a miserable, rotten, evil, asexual being.

Mary heard stories of her throughout her long career in home textiles. She avoided her at all costs. Most people did. Her first husband had several run-ins with her at his company and affectionately referred to her as the C word.

Nina walked past me on the way to her desk and whispered: "We're fucked." I nodded. She was right. Within minutes, a company-wide email was issued, announcing Joseph's departure and the restructuring. It all seemed so clinical. I deleted the email with a lump in my throat. We were definitely fucked.

Back at my apartment, I invited Jack over. I really didn't feel like being alone. Typically, I would have drowned my sorrows with a magnum of wine and ate my feelings through pizza and wings. I just wanted to vent.

"Fuck her," said Jack as we played *Grand Theft Auto*.

"I know. I wish you could see her in action. I've never met a bigger sociopath." Taking out my frustration by launching a rocket into the crowd, I smiled.

Jack shook his head. "Says the guy with the rocket launcher."

"Hey, this is my release. And besides, you introduced me to it."

"You have any food?" he said, setting down his controller and heading to my fridge. He helped himself to some leftover sesame chicken.

"What am I going to do?" I asked.

"Can you switch departments or something?" he said, eating the chicken cold, from the container, with his fingers.

"No. There's really nowhere I can transfer to. And there's no one really even in HR that I could talk to. They've all left or been fired." I said with a sigh.

"Maybe you could go wherever your old boss is going?" he said while I car-jacked a motorcycle.

"I don't think he's landed anywhere. I think he wasn't prepared for this."

"Quit."

"Yes, Jack. I will quit. And then what? Move in with you?"

"Just saying," he said, picking up his controller again.

"Would if I could." I set my controller down and picked up my wine. "Would if I could."

Train Boyfriends

"This is wrong," barked Patty as she dropped a stack of papers onto my hands as I was typing at my desk.

"What's wro…" I started to ask, but she had already turned on her bare feet, those disgusting, calloused, manly heels, and was off on a new terror mission. She probably has a small child to skin and eat, I thought. I pulled my hands from under the stack of paper to decipher what could be wrong with the report I prepared for her. I stayed until 10 o'clock the night before, triple checking all of my figures. After scouring it for a good five minutes, I discovered that the title row was only printed on the front sheet, not on every sheet, as she liked. I sighed and opened the spreadsheet and made the correction.

Patty brought back the report three more times, each with a thud on top of my hands. A period was missing. A word wasn't indented. A column was blue, not green. Around 9 o'clock, I think she just was tired of walking to my desk, so she went home. As soon as I had allowed for the requisite 15 minutes of her being gone, I left. Once, I had left right after her and she saw me in the lobby as she had forgotten something and returned to the office. She chewed me a new one, in full view of the security guards at the front desk. They still look at me with pity every morning as I enter through those shiny glass revolving doors.

I walked the long walk from the West Side Highway to the subway at 23rd and 8th. There was a slight nip in the air, but nothing I couldn't handle. I buttoned the top button on my jacket and wrapped my plaid scarf around me. A sense of relief blanketed me that I had survived another day. I could scratch another notch on my cell wall.

Despite its familiar smell of urine and wet towels, the subway station offered a warm relief from the night chill. I went through the turnstile and stood in my normal spot. Creature of habit. I looked around the platform. Just a couple other people. An older couple huddled together and a young girl carrying a hip curve and other necessary fashion designer tools. I recognized them immediately. FIT student, I thought. In a flash, I remembered back to when I was her, carrying those giant rulers, bags of muslin and giant sketch pads. I smiled.

I got on the train. No seats. I stood in the middle of the car and scanned it for this night's train boyfriend. It's a game I played to pass the time. I searched the car for the most beautiful man I could find and I claimed him as my boyfriend. I would stare at his handsome face and create an elaborate backstory about how we met, where we were just coming from and where we were headed.

One time I sat next to a chiseled Wall Street type. He was in a grey flannel suit, white shirt and solid baby blue satin tie. Very, 'Cary Grant', I thought. His chocolate brown hair, parted perfectly to the side and tucked behind his left ear. I named him Justin. He was just coming off a long day, I thought. He was leading the merger of two companies, a prospect six months in the making. He had finally closed the deal, pulling all-nighters for a week and the end had finally come. I could faintly smell alcohol on him. He probably had a celebratory drink at the office before leaving. He smiled at me as he sat down and immediately closed his eyes.

I pretended that we were on our way back to our townhouse in Brooklyn to change and go out and celebrate. I watched him peripherally and I could see that his eyes were still closed. Poor baby, I thought. Rich baby, I corrected myself with a chuckle. His head started to bob. He was seriously out of it.

All of a sudden, his head flopped in my direction and landed on my shoulder, where it stayed. The lady across from me looked at us with a smile. I made a shrugging gesture saying, I'm not about to wake someone so clearly tired. Station after station, he slept with his head on my shoulder. His hand was at my side, touching mine. I took my pinky finger and locked it in his and smiled. This beautiful, sleepy stranger was mine.

I flopped my head back against the window in bliss. For a second, I actually believed, *felt*, that we had dinner reservations waiting for us at our stop. Speaking of, I realized, that I had gone two stops past mine, and this guy had no indication that he was waking up any time soon. So, I sighed and rode all the way into Brooklyn. Instinctively, at the 7th Avenue stop in Park Slope, he raised his head, rubbed his eyes and apologized to me. I brushed it off, followed him out of the train, wished him well and got on the train back to Manhattan.

Another time, I saw a quirky looking blond guy with thick glasses. Not conventionally cute by any stretch, but there was something striking about him. I couldn't take my eyes off of him. I figured he had come from college, where we had given an art history lecture. One on art in the 21st century. He was going to meet up with his old college buddies for trivia night at the local bar and he had invited me to meet them. A big step in our relationship. I was nervous, I mean, what if I sucked at the trivia questions? Anything sports related and I was toast.

He noticed me staring at him and I quickly looked away, embarrassed. I looked back and he was still looking at me. I looked away again. I really sucked at this, I thought. What the hell, I will look one more time. He was still looking at me, this time he smiled. Without thinking I smiled back. My legs instantly felt like Jell-O. We stole a few glances and I stood staring at my feet. What was I going to do? This is uncharted territory for me.

I looked back and he was staring at my crotch and smiling. His eyes moved up and met mine and he gave me a wink. Suddenly, I felt cheap. I mean, I was looking forward to meeting his friends for trivia night.

He got up at the next stop, brushing his hand across my ass as he exited. He turned in the doorframe of the car and motioned with his head to follow him. I shook my head no. He shrugged me off and walked towards the exit. I slumped down in a newly open seat and felt so worthless. Why does no one want *me*?

Tonight, I looked around the car as I had done twice a day since I could remember. Patty and her antics were behind me. This was my time. I found a tall, handsome, young man standing at end of the car to my left. He had sandy blond hair slicked back, but not in a 'I use too much hair gel' sort of way. This was very cool. He had on a leather jacket and distressed jeans and was carrying a Prada briefcase.

He was coming from his advertising job. He was working with a startup firm and had just pitched a really cool idea for a soft drink ad. The senior partners green-lighted it and he was headed home to work on the project. I was meeting him at the station to go home with him so I could cook him dinner. I was going to make him my famous beef stew, his favorite. I would drop him off at the apartment and then I would run to the trendy wine shop around the corner and get his favorite wine, two bottles: one for us and one for the stew. And I would stop by the bakery and get a really crusty sourdough boule to mop up all the delicious stew. I would return to find him sitting behind his iMac, fast at work, printing ideas and pining them to the corkboard behind his desk.

I kissed the top off his head as I came in with the stuff for dinner and asked if he wanted a glass of wine. I poured him his glass before I started preparing our feast.

I looked up at him and he was smiling at me. I looked away quickly. I must have been lost in thought, staring at him and he smiled at me like aw, bless it, look at the special needs guy staring at me. I looked back and he was smiling at me. Again, my knees turned to Jell-O and I found it difficult to swallow. He looked at me and made a motion with his head to come down to his end of the car. Was this really happening? I was giddy like I hadn't been in a very long time.

I picked up my bag from the train floor and was about to head his way, when I felt someone breezing by me, their bag knocking my bag from my hand.

"Hello," said another beautiful guy to the guy who had been smiling at me.

"Hi," he replied. Suddenly, it was all so clear I was not the object of his affection. I turned and walked to the opposite end of the car so I wouldn't have to witness their first moments together. I got off at the next stop and started walking the rest of the way home.

Back at my apartment, I made myself my new favorite martini (half vodka, half gin with a splash of vermouth, shaken with a lemon peel) and sat down at my kitchen table and opened my PowerBook. For the duration of three martinis, I researched plastic surgery. After the fourth martini, I said "fuck it" and went to bed.

Stupid Me

I waited for Edward by the fountain in front of Lincoln Center. He was late for our date, but only by a few minutes. I bought us tickets to see "La Bohème" at the Metropolitan Opera. Kind of a lavish second date, but things had gone so well with him on our first that I really wanted to treat and impress him.

"Hey!" he said running up to me.

"Hey you," I said as he leaned in and kissed my cheek. He looked positively dashing in his tuxedo. He complemented me on mine. "There needs to be more black tie events in my life," I declared. He took my hand and we headed into the red carpeted and gold gilded world of The Met.

"This is so nice of you," he said as he sat down in his red velvet chair.

"You're welcome. I wanted to do something beyond dinner and a movie."

"This is certainly it!" I didn't really know if he liked opera. I did. I bought the tickets and then asked him if he wanted to go. I guess if he didn't want to, I could have dragged Sydney. She was a good sport that way.

After the second act, we went back out to the lobby area for the intermission. I bought us both a glass of champagne and we stood sipping it, looking at the chandeliers and the people in the lobbies below.

I looked at Edward and he smiled. He was shorter than me, solidly built and had a very kind face. Just thinking of his smile made me smile. "What are you thinking?" I asked.

"About kissing you."

"Oh, really?" I said, sipping my champagne out of nervousness. He nodded.

"Come here," he said, motioning for me to follow him. We went behind a column, where no one could see. He took my face with both of his hands and moved it to his. He gently and passionately kissed me. Pulling away, I sighed, keeping my eyes closed.

The chords indicating the next act was to start rang out, interrupting our make-out session. I followed him back into the hall, our hands locked. After Mimi had passed away and Rodolfo was left to grieve, we walked back out to the square in front of the complex. It was December and it was freezing out. But, that didn't stop us from walking around, hand-in-hand.

"Thank you for tonight," I said.

"No, thank you!" We found a bench by the pool opposite Avery Fisher Hall and sat down. We sat in silence and looked at the lights and the people rushing to get out of the cold. He took my hand put it in his pocket with his to warm them.

"These are the moments when I am so in love with New York."

"I know what you mean," he said.

We sat there in silence, keeping one another warm for about a half hour.

"Buy you a hot chocolate for the walk home?" I asked and he accepted. I knew of this really great street vendor that made the best hot chocolate. As luck would have it, he was still open. Sipping our warming beverages, I walked him to his apartment. He lived on the Upper West Side, so it really wasn't out of the way. "When can I see you again?" I asked boldly.

"Do you want to have dinner on Friday night?"

"Sounds like a date." He leaned in and kissed me just as he had at the opera. I desperately wanted to be invited it and kind of waited for it. But, he took his leave, ducking quickly into the warmth of his lobby. Probably just as well, I thought, we both have work tomorrow.

All week I couldn't wait to see him. We playfully sent emails and texts messages throughout the day and into the night. I loved all the attention he was showering on me. I never really thought of myself as a needy person, but I welcomed the adoration and affection.

Friday night we met after work at a small café in between both of our places of employment. He worked in Murray Hill as a tax accountant and my office was by the West Side Highway.

"So, glad the weekend is here," he said as we plopped down in a booth. He loosened his tie and sighed. Without thinking, I unbuttoned a button on my dress shirt.

"Yeah, this week was brutal. Looking forward to seeing you was what got me through." He smiled at me and picked up his menu. He ordered a half chicken and I opted for a burger and fries, tossing aside whatever diet I was following at the time. We didn't really speak during dinner. I think it was because we were both so exhausted from work and honestly, it was nice to have his company and not have to fill it with idle conversation.

After dinner, I asked him if he wanted to grab a drink or come back to my place. He opted for my place. Score! I thought. We were barely inside my apartment when we were undressing one another, our clothes in a pile on my kitchen floor. Completely naked, I led him into the bedroom and closed the blinds. Thank goodness, I picked up the apartment before I left for work, I thought. We stood at the foot of my bed, kissing each other passionately and exploring each other's bodies with our hands. Then came the most amazing sex.

We stayed in bed, exhausted, staring at the ceiling. "That was incredible," he said, catching his breath.

"Yeah, it really was." I think we fell asleep for a bit. When we woke, Edward had something to tell me.

"Hey, can I tell you something?" *Now?* Seems like that conversation should have happened already.

"Of course," I said braced for whatever was coming.

"I live with someone."

"Ok…" I said, drawing it out, waiting for the other part of this statement.

"It's my ex. We broke up months ago, but are locked in this lease and our rental company will not let us out."

"Ok…" I repeated.

"You have nothing to worry about," he said, rolling over and kissing me. "Trust me."

"Ok," I said. I wanted to trust him. I really did. I adored everything about him. His personality was perfect for mine, we had just enough in common and enough different to keep everything interesting and now I had discovered that the sex was amazing. If I just stuck it out for a few months, their lease would be up and he could get his own place. Or move in with me if we were at that point. "Ok," I said and reassured him with a kiss.

For the next two months, we continued to talk every day, saw each other at least once during the week and one weekend night he would stay over. We were settling nicely into a comfortable routine. He seemed happy. I was certainly happy with the way everything was shaping up.

Edward: *Dinner Friday night? At our usual café?*

I texted him back that we were on. Much of Patty's antics were lost on me since we met. My focus had shifted from caring about what she thought to putting my energy into my relationship with Edward. Even Jack remarked on the change. I went from bitching about Patty to gushing over Edward.

Friday night, I arrived early at the café. I took our normal booth and ordered a Diet Coke. He was late, but he was always late so I thought nothing of it. Our usual waiter placed two menus on the table and smiled.

My phone rang. It was Edward.

"Hello?" I said in a tone, asking if he was ok. He was crying. "Are you ok?"

"Kyle," he said sobbing.

"What is it? Are you hurt? Are you ok?" I panicked.

"I have to tell you something." My heart dropped straight down through me. "I…I…Last night, I slept with my ex." Tears welled up in my eyes. "Well, not exactly, but kind of."

"What do you mean?" I said, trying to mask my hurt.

"I came out of the shower and he was sitting on the floor in front of the sofa, jerking off to some porn. So, I joined him. We didn't touch one another and didn't kiss." I didn't know what to say. Silence hung out between us for several minutes. "I'm so sorr…"

"Don't," I cut him off. "Just don't." I hung up the phone and started bawling. He called back and I let it go to voicemail. He kept calling back and each time I sent it to voicemail. Finally, I just shut off my phone. I paid for my Diet Coke and left. Stupid, stupid me, I thought as I got on the train. I found a spot away from people and their pity. Stupid me.

The End of the Affair

Despite sitting five feet from one another, Nina and I were on Gchat. The office was open, fishbowl style and everyone knew everyone's business. It was our way of having a private conversation.

> Nina: I miss Joseph.
> me: I know. Me too.
> Nina: Patty is evil. She made Anne cry last week.
> me: I heard. Anne is what? Her third assistant in four months?
> Nina: Something like that.
> me: Do you think Joseph saw it coming?
> Nina: No, I think he was blindsided.
> me: Yeah, that fits Patty's style.
> Nina: Here she comes.

Quickly, we minimized our browsers. You could feel a wall of negative energy headed your way. It was like seeing a storm on the horizon and bracing yourself for it to hit.

"I need last year's selling on pillow inserts," she demanded, hands on her hips, bare foot tapping the perfectly white concrete floor. "Are you stupid? This is information you should have at the ready. What if I needed this for a board meeting or a touch base with the retailers? You've got to be fucking joking me!" she screamed at me. All of my coworkers turning to watch. My hands began to shake and panic began to wash over me. I was having trouble focusing my eyes and found breathing the hardest thing in the world.

"I just sent it to the printer," I said in a gasp as I finally came by the information. I ran and grabbed the printout.

"Don't you ever make me wait like that again," she said, ripping the paper from my hands, cutting open my index finger.

> Nina: Holy shit. I'm so sorry.
> me: I can't breathe.
> Nina: That was brutal.
> me: I'm going to the bathroom. I need a moment.

I propped myself up on the toilet at the last stall, the handicap stall, in the bathroom. I called it my 'office.' I sat there with my head between my legs, taking long, deep breaths. I braced myself with the bar on the wall next to the toilet. I closed my eyes. I'm ok. I'm ok. I'm ok. I kept repeating. Soon, the panic attack has passed. I was still paralyzed with fear, sitting, unable to return to my desk.

In a haze, I finally made it back to my chair.

> Nina: You ok?
> me: No. I just had the biggest panic attack.
> Nina: You want to go to 'wichcraft with me?
> me: Yes.

Sandwiches in hand, we found a little table and sat down. We ate for a bit without speaking.

"I can't believe I was just called stupid." My hands started to shake again at the thought of returning to work.

"What a day."

"And it's only noon."

Back at the office, I was girded for more of Patty's antics. I checked with Anne to get her schedule. A practice I began to follow every morning so I could pinpoint her location and either be prepared or conveniently absent. It was fairly easy to tell when she was headed your way because you could hear her shouting and see people ducking to avoid her. Marsha had a reputation, but she didn't frighten me the way Patty did. She was the devil.

"What is the gram weight of this submit?" she yelled, barefoot and heading my way.

"I don't know. It just arrived and wasn't labeled." And as a knee-jerk reaction, she grabbed a binder off the work island between Nina and my desks and threw it at me. I saw the big white binder headed in my direction, in slow motion, and was in such a state of disbelief that I didn't duck or flinch. It caught me right on the side of my face. The edge tearing open a small gash on my cheek.

Unapologetic, she screamed: "CALL THEM!" Blood starting to run down my cheek, I picked up the phone, fingers shaking and dialed our retail partner. My voice cracked as I asked for Marissa, my utility bedding counterpart on the retail side. "She's in a meeting," I said.

"GET HER!" Patty screamed and slammed her fist down on my desk, rattling my computer and knocked over my pen cup.

"I know she's in a meeting, but it's really urgent, can you please get her?" I begged her assistant. A few moments later I had my answer. "260 gsm," I said, hanging up the phone, noticing the blood on the handset for the first time. Patty let out a sigh and retreated to her office.

> Nina: You're bleeding.
> me: I know.
> Nina: I'm so sorry.

I grabbed the first aid kit I carry in my bag and went to my 'office.' I patched myself up and took a Klonopin. I had been left so traumatized by the recent events that I began seeing a therapist for the panic attacks and was promptly put on antidepressants and muscle relaxers. A much needed bridge to help get me across. I can't go back out there, I thought, thinking of all my coworkers watching me cower to her. Finally, I did.

> Nina: You could sue.
> me: I know. I just want this to end and Joseph to come back.
> Nina: Me too.

A text came across my phone from Sydney: *Buon Gusto at 8?* Precisely what I needed, another crutch to get me through the day. I don't know if secretly, somewhere in the inner depths of Patty, she felt guilt or remorse for throwing the binder at me, but I stayed out of her crosshairs for the rest of the day. 7:30 p.m. rolled around and I grabbed my bag and headed to dinner.

"What the fuck?" Sydney said as I approached her at the restaurant. I thought she was referring to the wound on my cheek, but I soon realized what she meant. *Buon Gusto* was gone. Well, the space was still there, but now it was painted a bright Grecian blue and the name was changed. Shocked, I opened the door and Sydney went in. Our beloved and sacred *Buon Gusto* was now a Middle Eastern restaurant. "I really wanted spinach tortellini," she said. "Hey, what happened to your face?"

My phone buzzed from inside my bag. I picked it up and looked. "This is what happened." I held out the phone to Sydney. I had put Patty in my phone as the C word.

"Yes, Patty?" I answered.

"Where are you?"

"At dinner. It's after 8."

"Get back here," she demanded.

"Is there something I can help with over the phone?" I said, trying to mitigate the situation.

"I need to see the revised sheeting samples."

"They are in a stack on the edge of my desk."

"You should be here," she said and slammed the phone down.

The next day, Patty was sitting at her desk as I was walking to my desk. "Get in here," she snipped.

I sat down, ready for her to deliver an apology. Sorry for screaming at me. Sorry for forcing me onto pills so I could survive the day. Sorry for the binder attack.

"I'm only going to tell you this once. If you see me in this office, you are to be in this office. In fact, I want you here before I come in and here after I leave. You got that?" I nodded, deflated further. She was now the Sun Queen. Everything rose and set with her.

> me: Where's Anne?
> Nina: Patty fired her after you left for dinner.
> me: You've got to be joking. How am I going to find her schedule now?
> Nina: No idea.
> me: Who is going to be the new Anne?
> Nina: No idea.

I washed a Klonopin down with a gulp of coffee. I could hear Patty yelling somewhere in the clerestory. I took another one.

This was my life for almost six months after Joseph left. The panic attacks, even with the medicine, didn't go away. Some mornings, I would have to get off the train a few stops before my normal one so I could find a bench and catch my breath. One morning, I blacked out on the train. Fell to the floor like I was instantly filled with lead. "You ok?" said a police officer who happened to be in the car. I explained that I was fine, didn't need to go to the hospital, that my boss would hang me in the clerestory if I were late. He asked what a clerestory was.

At night, I would lie in bed and cry and drink vodka straight from the bottle. I had never been in such a dark, hopeless place. Alana in HR had been long gone. I have no allies, I thought. During my tenure, the place had become a revolving door of talent. There were only a few generalists left in HR who filtered résumés and filled the same positions three or four times a year. Once a quarter, usually before the earnings announcement, there would be a round of layoffs so the company could realize a savings in payroll. Never mind that Marsha herself was syphoning money out of the company. Her multiple homes and the staff in them, her gardeners, her personal trainer, her masseur, her driver, her security guards, even a spending account for flowers and other incidentals were all paid for by the company. No one wanted to stand up to her and close her wallet.

What am I going to do? I thought. I should have been looking for a new job, but I had a sense of entitlement to my position. I was a huge Marsha Stuart fan. I had worked so hard to get my dream job and I wasn't about to let Patty get in the way of that. But, there was really no other open position that I could move into. What am I going to do? I asked again.

Getting off the elevator, I turned on the lights, unlocked the door, waved at the night receptionist/guard and went in. I started the coffee maker and turned on my computer. I kind of liked the morning by myself, even if it did mean getting up at 5 a.m. every day. It was my calm before the storm. Some mornings, I would sneak into Marsha's office, sunlight glimmering on the Hudson River, and remind myself of why I loved the brand.

Today was going to be a jam-packed day. We had an all-day meeting with the retailer and then an intense meeting with the president of the company where we presented our financial results and plans for the next season. Luckily, Patty took the lead in our meetings and nothing was thrown at me, verbal or physical. Maybe a page had been turned? Maybe I had finally proven myself to her?

Our company meeting went well, too. I presented my portion of the meeting with ease (thank you, Klonopin!). I sat back in my chair, in the executive conference room, and sighed. My day was done. As soon as the last presenter had finished, Janet, our company president cleared her throat. She was a skeleton really, with overly tan skin pulled to its limit over the frame. Her hair perfectly coifed into a twist/beehive hybrid. She was as equally frightening as Patty. They were friends, in fact. I often pictured them killing wild animals with their bare hands and drinking the blood and planning world domination.

"There will be another meeting following this one, in a half hour. When you get back to your desks, some of you will find the invite to that meeting. Those who don't, will be getting a separate meeting with your manager. That's all."

The room suddenly felt like it was draped in black fabric. No one spoke as they exited, everyone rushing back to their desks to see if they had the invite. I did the same.

> me: No invite. You?
> Nina: Yes.

"Kyle! In here! Now!" barked Patty one last time. "Shut the door." I sat down, braced for what was coming. "I don't know how to say this other than you're fired." I sat there motionless. It was as if the room was suddenly a vacuum in deep space. "You have a meeting with HR after this. Go to her to hand in your security card and get your exit paperwork." I stood up and I don't know why, but I thanked her. Looking back it was the oddest thing to do. I can only attribute it to an end of the suffering and I had been released.

> Nina: You ok?
> me: Yep. Bye.

I grabbed my bag, met with HR and I left. Patty's reign of terror was over. But, so was my association with Marsha.

I went home and began purging anything in my apartment with her name on it. Cookbooks, magazines, towels, that mirror. Looks like I was going to have to repaint.

This Little Light

"Dude," said Jack "I can really have this shit?" I nodded. I couldn't live with myself with dumping all my Marsha Stuart stuff in the trash. It seemed so wasteful to just throw it in the bins out front of our building. Jack's apartment, bless his heart, was challenged, to say the least, so I figured these items would find a good home there. And since Jack pretty much spent all his time in my apartment (because I always had food, booze and toilet paper), I would never have to see them again.

"My place is going to be so tricked out. Thank you," he said giddy like a kid on his birthday.

"No prob," I said, holding a half-burned Marsha Stuart candle, *Earl Grey Tea* scent. I studied it for a bit and said: "I'll keep this. It's half used anyway."

"Ok," he said, not caring as he was making out quite well minus one candle. I helped him carry his new home goods down to his apartment and left him to decorate. I climbed the stairs back to my place and lit the candle. My last Marsha Stuart item and I would be rid of her. Well, save the paint on my walls. Jack agreed to help me repaint as payment for his bounty.

I sat down at my kitchen table and looked for the couple across the way. They were out. I opened my PowerBook, answered a few emails, mainly to decline dinner and drink offers. I wasn't feeling very social after losing my job. Jack was the only person I could really stand to be around since he was a musician and not in the 9-6, M-F scene that the rest of my friends were in.

After deleting several credit card and male enhancement pill offers, I saw that my mom was begging me to return to Wisconsin for a visit. I shuddered. I couldn't fathom the thought of returning home, having lost yet another job. No way. Money! I'll use that as an excuse. She would never pay for my ticket so, that was my out. Jack sent me a thank you email. Why couldn't he just be gay? It would all be so easy.

What was I going to do next? What was going to be my 2.0? I had no idea. Was I just going to go on a string of ill-fitting jobs with bad bosses? Was that my lot? I sighed.

> Jack: Dude, I'm taking you out. To say thanks.
> me: Aw. That's ok.
> Jack: No, man, you can't say no.
> me: Ok, fine.

I set my phone down. I really didn't feel like being social, but it was Jack and getting out of my apartment probably would do me some good. I walked down the flight of stairs to his apartment, where I found him installing his new wares.

"This shit is so nice!" he said, setting a hurricane on his table. I never thought I would hear him say that. I busted out laughing. "What?" he said, then realizing the situation.

We ended up going to the bar/restaurant across the street. It had become our go-to place for food and drinks. We found a table near the back. The cute Asian waitress recognized us and greeted us warmly. There's perks to being a regular, I thought.

"Dinner's on me," he said proudly, handing me the menu.

"Nah, don't worry about it," I said. But, he heard none of it. I relented. We both scanned the menu despite both of us having it memorized. Our waitress leaned in and lit the candle in the votive in between us.

"Some candlelight for you," she said with a wink. I smiled at Jack. We loved teasing people who thought we were a couple. Which was often.

Jack never asked what I was going to next. He knew better. And that wasn't a concern of his. He wanted me to be happy, not hounding me with the usual questions. Our beers arrived and we cheered to new beginnings. I couldn't have felt happier.

After dinner, we made the long journey back across the street. "Are you going to kiss me goodnight?" I joked. "Come on! You should put out after I gave you all that stuff." He laughed. Back in my apartment, I re-lit the *Earl Grey Tea* candle on my table next to my favorite chair. I breathed in the scent and plopped down next to it. What was next?

The next morning, I awoke in the same position. I did manage to blow out the candle, but fell asleep in the chair. I never did that. I started the coffeemaker and opened my PowerBook, which was still on the kitchen table. I had the usual lot of emails wishing me well, job suggestions, and the like. I deleted them all. I poured myself a cup of coffee and watched the couple across the way preparing for their day.

I went to the website of the retailer that sold the Marsha Stuart goods I developed. It was torture to see items now for sale that I had worked on. I saw a quilt and thought of the time Patty threw a stack of Pantone chips off the work island because the color she was looking for was missing. I saw a lotion pump and remembered her making the vendor cry because the angle of the spout was wrong. There was the *Earl Grey Tea* candle. I thought of the time I was with Mary and Katie, in a small conference room with a thousand vials of fragrance, opening and closing them to choose candle scents. We were so high from the fumes, we were laughing at everything. I love candles, I thought. It was the one of the few good memories I had there.

Candles. I googled 'candle-making.' I read several different websites and blogs about how to make your own candles. I found a couple suppliers and ordered a starter kit of soy wax, lead-free cotton wicks, the wick tabs to secure them to the bottom of the glass, frosted glass vessels and pink grapefruit fragrance oil. I was ecstatic at the idea of actually making something. Since leaving college, I hadn't made one thing. Well, that wasn't for the apartment.

A few days later, the kit arrived and I went to work. I put the double-sided tabs on the end of the wicks and centered them in the bottoms of the vessels. I brought a stockpot of water to a boil (I again thought of Sydney and the chicken and smiled), measured out the soy wax into a stainless steel pitcher I ordered for this purpose, melted the wax, stirred in the fragrance and poured the candles. I sat at my kitchen table and watched the wax slowly cool. This is the coolest thing in the world, I thought. I sipped my coffee and marveled at what I had done.

I ordered more wax and fragrances so I could experiment. *Fresh Cut Grass, Tuberose, Gardenia, Campfire, Atlantic, Peppermint, Asian Sandalwood.* I loved choosing fragrances. I found interesting vessels from a different source, even designed my own labels in Adobe Illustrator on the computer and had them professionally printed. I found a box supplier and got those, as well. Soon, I had a little candle factory set up in my kitchen. *Kyle Meyers Home Collection*, I had dubbed my brand. I had plans to expand beyond candles and the designation made it sound like I had more products than I did. I liked it.

"What are you going to do with all those candles?" asked Jack as he played *Grand Theft Auto*. I had given him several to test. They passed.

"Sell them, I guess," I said and immediately searched for a place to sell them. *Etsy*! Duh! So, as Jack played the video game, I set up my storefront. All of this happened so effortless and quickly. I went from unemployed Product Manager to candlemaker extraordinaire.

My first order came through for a *Lemon Verbena* candle. I sat with the biggest grin on my face as I looked at the email informing me of the order. I printed it and stuck it to the fridge to always remind myself of this order, this beginning.

I raced to ship the candle and was hungry for my next order. Which came the next day. Steadily, the orders increased and soon my warehouse of candles was almost depleted. I ordered more supplies and replenished my stock. I was on to something.

Eight weeks after starting my candle business, I received an email from a store in D.C. that wanted to carry my candles. We reached an agreement on wholesale price and quantities and I started shipping them down to the store. They sold out immediately and a reorder was placed.

This really was a bright idea.

Rapey the Clown

"Kelly!" I exclaimed, noticing her in the crowd. Still dressed in all black, but there was an edge to her that was no longer there.

"Oh, my God, Kyle!" It had been forever since we had seen one another. We immediately hugged. "What are you doing in town?" She and her boyfriend, Martin, had moved to Westchester a few months prior.

"I'm here on a job interview. With a toy company."

"Excellent. Are you coming or going?"

"Just coming from. It went ok."

"What position?" I asked.

"Senior designer."

"That would be perfect for you!"

"I know! What about you?"

"Oh, I was just out getting some sewing supplies." I held them up as proof.

"Say, let's get a drink. I've been dying to see what *Buon Gusto* has turned into." It was 3 o'clock. Why not? We headed down in the direction of our former haunt.

"How are things with Martin?" I asked.

"Great! Things are going so well."

"Cohabitation is working out?"

"Couldn't be better." I smiled. We walked the rest of the way in silence. Kelly and I had a knack of picking back up where we left off if we had lapsed in our communication. Since her move, we spent our days gchatting, keeping one another company. "This is it?" she said, viewing the new Middle Eastern restaurant *Buon Gusto* had become.

"I know. Sydney and I feel the same way." We went in and sat at the bar. I ordered a Campari and soda and Kelly a gin and tonic. We surveyed the room. The crowd seemed seedier than before. And that was a stretch because it was already pretty much a blue-collar bar.

"Kinda sketchy now," Kelly said.

"See what happens when you leave?" I joked with her.

"No shit." On the edge of the bar was a stack of ice breaker, conversation starter cards. I picked one up: "What scares you?" it read. I handed it to Kelly for her response. "Hmm. Let's see. Heights. Or falling from a great height. Definitely. You?"

"Clowns. I have the biggest, irrational fear of clowns." Kelly set the card down and took out her notebook where she had sketched a clown. She showed it to me. "That clown is pretty tame looking." She started revising his drawing, making him look more haggard and beat up. She added an empty scotch bottle to his hand, made his makeup run, put tears in his costume and his wig was set ajar. "He looks rapey now." We busted out laughing.

"That's what I am calling him, Rapey the Clown."

"He needs a windowless van that he rides around in." Kelly went to work. She drew a beat up old mini-van without windows. "Make the sides airbrushed." She spit out her drink a little, luckily not on our masterpiece. She drew a unicorn scene on the side of the van and erased the hubcaps. I busted out laughing.

"He needs candy canes stuck to the dashboard." Those were added. We then created an elaborate backstory for Rapey. He had lost his job at the cannery for taking too many cigarette breaks and stealing cans of corn at the end of his shift. (Kelly added a pile of empty tin cans around the back door of the van.) Rapey had found a clown costume at the Salvation Army and started his own business from his van. Which was also his home. He started showing up to his birthday parties and bar mitzvahs reeking of alcohol. He soon became less and less in demand, but refused to take off his costume.

The bartender, a very Goth looking girl, asked us if we wanted to see the food menu. Sure, we said. I ordered a chicken shawarma salad and Kelly opted for hummus and pitas. As we ate our food, we came up with various titles for Rapey. Kelly grabbed a stack of cocktail napkins and went to work.

Rapey Does Hard Time

Rapey Gives His First Blowie

Rapey The Drug Mule

Rapey Shops For A Dookie Suit

Rapey Tries Fisting

Kelly quickly sketched covers for each of these book ideas. We were giggling like middle school kids being naughty. The bartender at the end of the bar, shaking her head at us. We didn't care.

The door opened and the little bell affixed to the top of it rang out another patron had arrived. It was this Tammy Faye looking woman in a black leather halter top, black patent leather hot pants, black fishnet stockings and 6-inch stiletto heels. Her hair was jet-black and teased to within an inch of its life. She stumbled up to the bar and set her giant patent leather bag on the stool next to her.

"Oh, dear Lord," I whispered to Kelly. We couldn't take our eyes off her.

"That's the dominatrix. Her name is Maxine. She used to come into *Buon Gusto* all the time," Kelly whispered.

"How did I never see her?" I whispered back.

"Mommy needs a tequila," she ordered in her smoky, raspy voice. The bartender must have known her and without instruction, took the bottle of Patron Silver off the self and poured her three shots. After slamming them, she let out a guttural sigh, ending with a belch.

"Well, I'm no longer hungry," I said, pushing my plate forward. Kelly was still drawing. "You know, you should really do a children's book. Or a coloring book. You are an excellent illustrator."

"You think?" she said stopping to look at me.

"Yes! I say you do it."

"I think I might." And with that, we started outlining non-Rapey, non-pedophile clown stories that she could turn into coloring books. Our childishness actually generated a real idea. I asked though, if I could keep the Rapey drawings for my fridge. Kelly kept "Rapey Buys Anal Beads" for herself.

"Time to settle up," Maxine snarled. She was clearly shit-faced. She was having trouble locating her wallet in that big patent leather bag. Out of frustration, she took the bag and dumped its contents on the bar. Dildos of every shape, size and color spilled out and fell everywhere. Pink ones, curved ones, even a large black one with a horse's tail attached to it. The fall triggered several to start buzzing and vibrating and a couple even started blinking and glowing. "Oh, fuck," Maxine said as she fumbled to turn them off and put them back in her bag. The two that had fallen behind the bar were thrown back up on the bar and the bartender ran to the sink and washed her hands four times.

Having thrown money on the counter, Maxine stood up and fell backwards a little, one of her razor pointed stilettos breaking off. "Oh, shit!" she exclaimed, catching herself on the barstool. She slung her big black bag over her shoulder and leaned in for a whiff. "Mommy needs a bath. Smells like I've been sitting in hot dog water." Kelly pushed her plate forward and gagged a little.

"You can't make this shit up," I said as Maxine hobbled out the door.

Love Is All Around

"I met someone!" Sydney said, ripping open a sugar packet and putting it in her coffee.

"Really? Details!" I said, sipping mine.

"His name is Drew. He is getting his biology degree. We met at a party that Jocelyn threw. You remembered her?" I shook my head. "She was in Fashion Design with us. Always made those skirts our professor said would serve better as belts?" Still wasn't jogging my memory. "Anyway, she had a housewarming party for her place in Spanish Harlem and I met him there."

"That's cool," I said, looking over the brunch menu.

"When are we going to find you someone?"

"Isn't that the question of the ages?" Our waiter came and took our order.

"Oh, my God! I've got it! I'm setting you up with my friend Keith from work!"

"What do you know about Keith?"

"Well, he's funny and you'd like him."

"So, basically, you know one gay person and for that reason I should date him." She shot me a disapproving look. "Ok, fine. Give Keith my number."

"Yay!" she said joyfully, excited about her new role as matchmaker.

My phone vibrated on the table. I picked it up. It was from Kelly.

Kelly: I'm getting married! Martin just proposed!

Me: OMG, congrats! Best news ever.

"Kelly's getting married." I said, setting my phone back down.

"What the fuck? Are you serious?"

"Yup," I said.

"Wow. I didn't see that one coming."

Martin was a studious, tall, trim black guy that Kelly met at a party. He worked as a film editor for a production company. He completed and complemented Kelly in the best way. We had all gone out to dinner after they started dating so we could meet him. We all fell in love with him, too. But, Kelly was wildly opposed to marriage and what it stood for so it was a surprise that she said yes.

We finished our brunch and started walking down 5th Avenue. "When am I going to meet Drew?" I asked.

"Well, at Kelly's wedding, I guess."

"Not until then?"

"We're still getting to know one another!"

"Ok, ok. No worries," I said, bumping into her on purpose.

"When Keith calls, answer it please!" I was known to let phone calls go to voicemail.

"Ok," I said.

That night I sat at my kitchen table, eating stir-fry I had made. My floor was vibrating and I could hear Jack below working on new songs. Normally, the sounds would bother me, but it was comforting knowing he was there, creating. It was like having company that I didn't have to entertain.

I scanned through several job boards, but nothing looked appealing to me. The thought of entering another horrible work situation made me cringe. I was completely threadbare, like a beaten up puppy. But, my candle business was booming and I didn't really need the income. The benefits would be great, but was I willing to forego them in order to be my own boss?

I watched a sparrow land on the fire escape outside my kitchen. He seemed so happy, just hanging out there on the railing. Jack repeated the same chorus over and over. He must have been on to something. Sounded like a love song. I would have to ask him to make me a copy of it when it was finished.

An electronic invite came through as a save the date for Kelly's wedding. That was quick, I thought. They were getting married in the summer. I liked that she wasn't drawing out her engagement for a year or longer. There was nothing worse than hearing about the minutiae of someone's wedding for over a year as they planned it. That wasn't Kelly's style anyway. I entered it into my calendar so I wouldn't forget. Not that my calendar was chocked full of appointments.

I went over to the TV and flipped through my Netflix discs. I put a DVD in the player and sat down on the sofa and threw my pale blue throw over my legs. About twenty minutes into the movie, my phone rang. It was a number I didn't recognize.

"Hello?" I hesitated.

"Ky-le?" the person slurred.

"This is he," I said.

"This is Keith." He was clearly drunk. I could almost smell the alcohol through the phone.

"How are you?" I mustered, trying to mask my annoyance.

"I'm goo-ood!" he said with a chuckle. I bet he was.

"Great," I said. We sat in the most uncomfortable silence.

"Whatcha doin'?" he slurred and stumbled. I heard him knock into something.

"Watching TV. You?"

"Just having a drink at my place."

"Great," I said with zero emotion.

"You want me to come over? We could have some fun!" He hadn't even seen a photo of me. At least, not unless Sydney had shown him one.

"Aw, that would be great, but I have to get up early tomorrow. Big day at work."

"Another time then!" And with that we said goodbye. I hoped he didn't find out I wasn't working. Then again, I doubt he would even remember calling me. I picked up my phone and texted Sydney: "Do not set me up again."

I stopped my Netflix disc, took it out and put in *Brief Encounter*, the old Noel Coward film. I shut off the lights, lit a candle, pulled the blanket up over me and let out a sigh. Why was finding a man so difficult? A good one, that is.

A Wedding and a Birth

"How do I look?" Kelly asked, nervously, standing in front of a full-length mirror.

"You're beautiful," I said.

"I can't believe I'm getting married."

"You?" I said, gently punching her bare arm. "I thought a man on Mars would have happened sooner." She punched me back.

It was true. I never thought that Kelly would get married. The gruff, chain-smoking bartender was now living in the suburbs, drawing children's coloring books. Who would have predicted that?

"How did the book go?" I asked, flopping down in the chair next to her. She immediately ran with the idea of penning one of her own after my suggesting it.

"Paid for this wedding."

"Nice!" I said as she pivoted from side to side, inspecting her gown. I was happy for her. It was weird to not see her in black. Normally, I loathed weddings and avoided them at all costs. Kelly and Martin were perfect together and I wanted to be no place on Earth but there, celebrating with her. It didn't even bother me that I was there without a date. Well, Jack was kind of my date.

Kelly's mom stuck her head in the door, twinkling with pride. "Ten minutes, sweetie!" she said. Kelly nodded with a smile.

"I'm going to go get my seat." I said, kissing her gently on the cheek. "You really look beautiful."

The wedding venue was the Sunset Terrace at Chelsea Piers. It was at the end of the pier on the Hudson River with the most amazing views of New Jersey and the sun setting on the horizon. Half the space was set up as the wedding area and the other was the reception space. My kind of wedding: zero travel from church to hall.

I found my gold colored banquet chair and took my seat. Sydney and her man, Drew, were there, across the aisle from me. She leaned forward and waved. I waved back. She pointed at Drew with the biggest grin on her face. I threw her a thumbs-up sign and a big smile.

"Dude," Jack said, leaning in to whisper in my ear. "I'm going to mack on so much here."

"Seriously? Did you just say that?" I said. He did have a point, the single girl to guy ratio was definitely in his favor.

Martin stood at the end of the aisle, in front of us all, with only the priest next to him. No bridesmaids or groomsmen. This was definitely my kind of wedding. He looked so handsome in his tuxedo. I could tell he was standing on the tips of his feet, then down, and then back on the tips. I smiled at his nervousness. What was to be nervous about? He was marrying one of the most beautiful and funny and intelligent women I had ever met!

And there she was. Kelly appeared, on cue to the music. We all stood and watched her walk towards Martin. She looked my way and winked. She was radiant. I wanted to jump out in the aisle and hug her. After the wedding, I thought.

I could make out the Statue of Liberty, just over Martin's shoulder. The sunset was casting a beautiful golden color over all of us. I took a deep breath and sighed a long sigh. In a very simple and quick ceremony, Kelly and Martin were married. We all jumped up and cheered at them. I got teary eyed and wiped them away quickly so Jack wouldn't notice and tease me.

As photos were snapped of the couple, the wedding area was converted into a dance floor and the DJ set up his equipment. We all went to the bar area and got whatever cocktail our hearts' desired. I went for my standby and got a Campari and soda. I stood with Jack, who got a whiskey sidecar, surveying the room.

"You are going to do quite well tonight," I said.

He clinked his drink to mine. "Here's hoping," he said with a grin. God, I loved his grin.

Sydney and Drew made their way to us. "Kyle, this is Drew," she introduced us. I shook Drew's hand. Not what I had expected. Sydney usually went for the tattooed bad boys. Drew looked very straight-laced and nerdy. More my type than hers. "Can you believe Kelly is married?" she asked, sipping her Jack and Coke.

"You're next," I said. Drew choked on his drink. I took a sip of my drink and noticed Jack was gone. The DJ played A-Ha's "Take On Me." People were dancing a little in the bar area, while others sat down at their assigned seats in the dining area. "How's your Etsy shop going?" asked Sydney grabbing a mini quiche off a tray as a waiter passed by.

"Unbelievably well." It was true. I had added hand-embroidered kitchen towels, dinner napkins, cocktail napkins, pillow covers and even goat's milk soaps and room sprays. I was generating enough orders to pay my rent and keep ordering supplies. No longer was I under the shackles of a bad boss. No longer was I at someone's judgment of my résumé. I spent my days at my kitchen table sewing, packaging items, shipping orders. My apartment was now design studio, workshop and warehouse. It was bliss.

"Too bad the reception couldn't have been at *Buon Gusto,*" said Sydney with melancholy. Suddenly, I was craving tortellini with Alfredo sauce. I nodded in agreement.

"What do you do, Drew?" I asked.

"I'm a research scientist."

"Very cool," I said, not sure of what to ask him next.

"Let's dance," said Sydney, pulled Drew out to the dance floor. I smiled and took a sip of my Campari.

The room smelled of flowers and the candlelight and string-lights cast a warm glow on everything. I found my seat at table 5 and surveyed the room. There was so much happiness in one space. It was impossible to not feel it. Sydney and Drew danced a little and it made me smile. Mainly because he was a foot shorter than she and they were having trouble keeping time. As odd as it appeared, they seemed perfect for one another. I noticed Jack dancing with a pretty blond girl in a purple strapless dress. I think she was one of Kelly's cousins. That didn't take long. "Good luck to you," I said to him in my head with a chuckle. Kelly and Martin danced slowly, whispering to one another, unaware of the guests around them.

I felt something in the breast pocket of my jacket. It was my broken compass. I must have left it in there after a job interview, I thought. I set it on the table and smiled. I tore off a piece of bread from the basket in front of me and slowly chewed it. I looked around the room and for the first time in my life, I felt ok.

The End

About the Author

Jamie Godfrey is author and entrepreneur. When he is not jotting down his quirky musings, he is the owner/designer of Jamie Godfrey Home Collection. There he sells a range of handmade home goods. He also enjoys cooking, decorating, playing the piano, Grand Theft Auto and drinking Campari. West of Me is Jamie's first novel. He currently lives in Jersey City, NJ.

www.ingramcontent.com/pod-product-compliance
Lightning Source LLC
Chambersburg PA
CBHW050934120626
46552CB00001B/206